As the lights bounced off the shiny ornaments of the Christmas tree, Tess felt a little bit of the spirit of the season. For a moment she stood, watching the tree, enjoying the flash and the glow the colors.

A yawn reminded her she needed to be back upstairs in bed. She moved toward the tree slowly, trying to figure out where the plug was so she could turn off the lights. Finally she knelt beside the tree and began to push the branches back, searching for the cord.

Her eyes widened when she touched something solid beneath the tree. Surely no one had put a present there yet.

Grasping one of the lower branches, she pulled it back so that she could view the area beneath the tree.

She found herself looking into Nathan's eyes. They were frozen and glazed, offering back a stare of nothingness.

For a second Tess tried to figure out how he'd managed to get into such an odd position.

Then she realized that only his head was there.

Other books by Sidney Williams

Horror Novels and Collections
Azarius
Blood Hunter
Gnelfs
Night Brothers
Scars and Candy
When Darkness Falls

Thriller Novels
Dark Hours
A Disturbance of Shadows (forthcoming)
Midnight Eyes

Si Reardon Series
Fool's Run
Long Waltz

Sci-Fi/Fantasy Novels
Disciples of the Serpent: A Novel of the O.C.L.T

Young Adult Horror
Dark Angel Christmas
Deadly Delivery
New Years Evil
The Gift

NEW YEAR'S EVIL

SIDNEY WILLIAMS
WRITING AS MICHAEL AUGUST

One

Candles

Wax World, the candle shop, was located on a quiet corner just off Main Street in downtown Pembrook. As a light autumn rain fell from dust-colored clouds, Tess Ryan pulled her mom's old Buick Century to a stop against the curb.

The engine clanged and clattered as she shut off the ignition, but she'd learned not to worry about the sounds the old car made. It wasn't a BMW, but it gave her enough freedom to get around, and it hadn't failed her yet.

Her access to reliable transportation was part of why she'd been elected for this mission. Pulling the hood of her slicker over her head to protect her long brown hair, she popped the door open and slipped out of the car. She sprinted for the front of the shop, where an awning stretched over the entrance. Once she made it there she was safe, at least from the storm.

Before reaching for the knob, she turned to look at the front windows. They offered a sharp contrast to the bleakness of the day. On one side, fake snow had been sprayed around the glass, creating a white border which framed a display of Christmas candles.

Cheery elves and Santas stood behind the glass in a field of cotton snow, their hands offering up red and green candles and bits of holly. A large candle shaped like Santa's sleigh stood behind them, and candy cane candles were posted further back.

The other window was filled with paper turkeys and Pilgrims as well as brown candles, but Thanksgiving was only a couple of days away. More elves would probably evict the Pilgrims in a couple of days.

Both of the exhibits were beautiful, but, as she'd expected, what she needed wasn't on immediate display. She'd have to shop a little inside.

She grasped the old door knob and twisted it, shoving the glass door inward and setting off a rattle of bells that echoed through the store's narrow front showroom.

There wasn't much floor space, and the room was made even more cramped by the large number of items Mrs. Tannenberry kept on hand. Large wax Santas stood like red sentinels on either side of the entrance, while huge white candles shaped as North Pole palaces were placed against one wall.

Small tables and multi-tiered shelves were placed at the center of the room, and they were filled with dozens of small candles in all shapes, sizes, and colors.

Tess felt a little nervous as she moved forward. She could hear Mrs. Tannenberry shuffling around in the back, obviously not in any hurry to respond to the bells.

That was fine with Tess. She just wanted to take a quick look around, find what she'd come for and depart. If she could locate the candles she wanted and plop down the cash, Mrs. Tannenberry wouldn't have time to ask questions.

Unfortunately, when people came in, Mrs. Tannenberry usually wanted to talk.

Quickly, Tess moved to the store's back wall. Small, red wooden buckets were set up there to hold short, scented candles, and beside those, more shelves displayed tapers in various colors.

She quickly began a search. White candles were along the bottom shelf. Red and green came next, and above the green were peach and other pastel colors. She frowned. None of those were right.

Turning, she looked around for other displays. There had to be candles like she needed. There had to be. As she often did when thinking, she raised her right index finger to her mouth and began to bite softly. It was a habit she'd tried to break, one her mother hated, but so far nothing short of electroshock therapy had helped. She'd been doing it since she was a kid, and now she was seventeen. Maybe she'd never get rid of it.

And maybe she'd never find the right candles.

"This weather is something isn't it?"

2

The voice made her turn with a start, but she sighed as she saw Mrs. Tannenberry framed in the stockroom doorway. She looked like she was ready to step into a Christmas display herself. With her white hair pulled back in a bun and her wire rimmed glasses, she could've stood beside Santa and posed as his wife.

"Can I help you?"

"I was just looking for something," Tess said, almost hesitantly.

"Candles I hope," Mrs. Tannenberry said moving into the showroom. She was carrying a box filled with red and green candles crafted to look like elves.

"Yes, candles," Tess said, continuing to look around. "Got lots of them."

But none of them were right. Tess continued to bite at her finger.

"What can I help you find? Need some Christmas candles? I've got some new ones that are shaped like Rudolph."

"I needed something different."

"Tea candles? Tapers?"

"Tapers, I guess. But the ones over there are the wrong color."

"Well what color do you need? I've got most everything. Red, green, mauve..."

"Black."

"Black? Hmm. That's not a very romantic color."

"It's not for dinner or anything."

"Oh, I thought somebody as pretty as you would be wanting them for dinner with her boyfriend."

Tess blushed. She'd been told she was pretty. She had an almost heart-shaped face with high cheekbones and deep brown eyes, but she never really considered herself beautiful. She wasn't cheerleader material, so she didn't regard herself as flashy.

Her mom sometimes accused her of being too cerebral, and maybe that was true. Maybe she was guilty of thinking too much and, by default, worrying too much.

Maybe that was true now. What did Mrs. Tannenberry care what color she wanted? Tess wasn't acting suspicious.

The old woman might think it strange Tess wanted black candles, but she wasn't going to immediately assume Tess wanted them for illicit

3

purposes. Who could suspect her real reason for the purchase? It was almost too unreal for her to believe.

"It's a school project," she lied, surprised at how easily the untruth passed her lips.

"Oh, I thought Thanksgiving vacation was on."

"Well, it started this week, yes, but they still give us homework."

"They ought to let you have some time to relax. Ridiculous that they'd give you projects over Thanksgiving." She heaved a heavy sigh. "Black candles. Let me see."

Disappearing through the doorway into the stockroom again, she returned in the blink of an eye with another red bucket.

"These are all I'm going to have that are black," she said, taking one candle out too give Tess a look.

It was one of the short, scented style, thick but no more than an inch and a half high. Tess felt her shoulders sag. It would have to do.

"These are sandalwood," Mrs. Tannenberry said sniffing the one she was holding and then extending it. "Used to be they made perfume like this. Bet you're way too young to remember that."

"Yes, ma'am," Tess said, accepting the candle and inhaling their almost too-sweet scent. That was going to be just perfect.

She wondered if scented candles would work. Did smells matter? Would they screw things up? All she could do was get the candles and check with Charisse.

"How many would you like?"

"Give me a dozen of them," Tess said.

"My goodness, it must be a big project."

"It's a massive one," Tess said, tugging a ten-dollar bill from her purse. It was her allowance, and she had other things she could spend it on, but this was her contribution to the plan.

The plan? That was a nice name for it. She couldn't believe what they were talking about doing. Maybe the plot was a better word for it.

A queasy feeling twisted around in her stomach as she reconsidered. Didn't they say there were some forces that were better left alone?

Charisse Bienville was supposed to be an expert. Rumor had it she was from New Orleans originally, and that was just one of the rumors about her.

As. Mrs. Tannenberry folded wrapping paper around the candles and tucked them into a bag, Tess thanked her. Forcing a smile, she then quickly turned to go before the older woman could ask any more questions.

She had to hurry. The others would be expecting her, and Charisse might get impatient. The girl had asked that everyone be on time, and, as she had been quick to point out, she was doing them a favor. Again that didn't seem quite the right word. Flipping her hood up, Tess made a quick dash for the car.

The Bienvilles had moved into the old Mullivan place, and it was on the edge of town, which meant she had a bit of a drive.

Tess couldn't imagine why they wanted to live there. They were supposed to be fixing it up, but it was a spooky, old two-story built heaven only knew when.

Nathan Drake had heard somewhere that the Bienvilles were distantly related to the Mullivan's, but that wasn't confirmed.

None of that mattered, she realized, as she turned the car at the corner of McMahon Street, then followed it to the turn at the water tower, where city workmen were already hanging strands of Christmas lights.

What mattered was getting this business over with.

Safe might be questionable, but everybody had agreed it was necessary. Something had to be done about Bran Hatten.

He'd harassed just about everybody at Pembrook High at one time or another. Heaven help the girl who refused to go out with him or the guy who crossed his path.

He had insulted and harassed both Tess and her friend S.W. after they had declined dates. There was no way to prove he'd done it, but the morning after she'd turned him down for the homecoming dance, S.W. had found a dead rat in her locker. A thin, nylon cord had been coiled around its neck, and it had dangled from a hook when she'd opened the locker door just before first period.

Tess hadn't received a gross-out after she'd turned him down for a date to see a Tom Cruise movie. He'd only knocked her lunch tray out of her hands in the cafeteria. She stood there with mashed potatoes on her jeans and peach juice running over her Reeboks, while he'd claimed it was an accident.

The whole student body had seemed to be watching and laughing at her.

Guys were treated a little differently. Silas Taylor, who was a pretty cool guy, had worn a shiner for almost a month after Bran slammed an elbow into his face in the crowded school hallway. No one had seen it in the rush of people, but the incident had occurred just after Silas had argued with Bran over some inane topic.

Bran had terrorized Nathan Drake for half the semester, sometimes making snide remarks but mostly just intimidating him with stern gazes. Nathan was not a big guy, and no match for Bran's bulk.

Just thinking about Bran got Tess steamed. His attitude almost made it seem justifiable—what they were talking about doing.

S.W. had been the first who'd noticed that Bran left Charisse alone. At first they'd decided it was because she was new at school this fall and hadn't had time to catch his eye.

Tess remembered the day that notion had changed. Tess had been heading for gym class, and Bran had almost knocked her down as he'd clomped past in his combat boots.

A few feet ahead, Charisse had been walking also, moving slowly and looking out the windows, which stretched along the corridor and overlooked the athletic field. She'd seemed to be lost in her own world and oblivious even to the heavy footfalls behind her.

Tess had watched, wondering if Bran was going to bulldoze Charisse as well. The red-haired girl had been blocking his path and moving at what he had probably viewed as an irritatingly slow pace.

Tess had winced as he moved forward, anticipating that he might do more than just push past Charisse. If the whim hit him, he might elbow her into the hall or trip her and pretend it was an accident.

Preparing to call out a warning, Tess had clenched her books like a shield. She hadn't wanted Bran to turn on her, but she hadn't wanted him bullying someone who had yet to learn to watch out for him.

She'd caught her words just before they'd rolled along her tongue because when he'd come only inches from Charisse, Bran had suddenly veered right, making a broad sweep across to the opposite side of the hallway.

He'd glided on past Charisse and moved onward as if pushed by a tailwind. Tess had picked up her pace then, falling in line with the new girl.

"You know Bran Hatten almost steamrolled you," Tess said. "Guess he changed his mind at the last moment."

"Did he, do you think?" Charisse had asked with a cool tone.

"Well, he came close."

Charisse had cocked one eyebrow and pursed her lips in an expression that had seemed both knowing and mysterious.

"You know, not everything is happenstance or coincidence," the red-haired girl had said. "Nature and the universe have their order, though it's an order that can be controlled."

She had pushed on then without another word, but she'd planted a seed. Tess had felt odd in her presence, as if she had brushed against the breath of eternity.

When she told S.W. what had happened, they agreed to keep an eye out to see if they could figure out what was going on.

The seed was nurtured over the following weeks.

After observing Charisse awhile, they decided she possessed something more. Bran noticed her, and he seemed to avoid her. There was something eerie about the flame-haired girl, something the kids whispered speculations about even though no one had any definitive answers.

On occasions when they spoke to her, she remained vague, yet she hinted at possibilities, tantalizing possibilities where Bran was concerned.

Finally, S.W. and Tess agreed to approach her, to ask outright what made Bran leave her alone. She didn't answer, just smiled knowingly.

"If you want to find out," she said, "I'll help you."

She then proceeded to mention things that would be needed and set this afternoon as a time to get a group together.

Tess shuddered as she considered what was about to happen. Charisse had promised that Bran soon wouldn't be bothering anybody ever again.

Two

Spellcasting on a Wet Afternoon

The house sat back off the road, partially concealed behind a cluster of old oak trees. As Tess pulled her car onto the winding driveway, she realized again how creepy the place looked, like something out of a horror movie.

The twisted branches, now almost barren of leaves, stretched like withered gray fingers across the high roofline and tapped against the panes of arched windows on the top floor. A dinginess seemed to hover over the house, the once-white paint now a faded gray, which confirmed the many passing years since its construction.

As she shoved the Buick's gearshift into park, she found herself hesitant about entering, and not just because of the eerie atmosphere. She still felt an apprehension about the planned proceedings of the afternoon.

Bran probably deserved whatever might happen, but were they ready for this? Were they this desperate? She'd heard many stories about how dangerous it could be to dabble with the unknown.

Tess didn't like confrontations or challenges. She considered firing the engine to life and getting out of there, but then she noticed The Judge, Casey's old, maroon Plymouth, which his father had helped him restore. It was one of the big, old-style models from the fifties, and the license plate read "Antique." It was parked at the end of the drive, partially hidden by the house. She'd almost been hoping that it would have broken down, as it often did. After all, Casey was the most likely to walk out, being something of a skeptic.

The others would have ridden with him, so they would all be inside, waiting. Tess couldn't walk out on them now. They were all counting on her.

Slowly, she climbed out of the car, picked up the bag of candles, and headed for the front door. Gnarled brown leaves covered the front lawn, and they rustled and crunched under her feet as she moved. The sound was almost loud enough to wake the … but she didn't want to think about that.

The old door was weathered, and the paint had begun to crack and peel. An old-fashioned twist bell was set into the door facing, and she turned the crank, sounding a grinding ring.

A second later, as if she'd been anticipating the approach, Charisse pulled the door inward.

Wind from the afternoon swept over her as she stood in the doorway. Her long red hair billowed back over her shoulders like tongues of flame, and her green dress fluttered around her slender frame. She was unquestionably beautiful, especially with her ivory skin as smooth as satin and her jade eyes flecked with gold. Tess felt like a scrub maid in her presence.

"Hello," Charisse said without inflection. "We've been waiting for you."

Tess pulled her jacket around her as another burst of wind swept across the lawn. "Sorry. I had to have Mrs. Tannenberry pull the candles out of stock."

"Come in."

She followed Charisse through a narrow entry hall into a parlor where the others were sitting. The room was a Victorian postcard with ornate, old chairs and a love seat along one wall.

Tess was a little put out with the arrangement. Nathan was sitting in one of the chairs, while Casey and S.W. were sharing the love seat. The narrow lounge forced them to sit much closer than Tess would have preferred.

Tess had no claim to Casey, at least not yet, but S.W. knew Tess was interested in him. She didn't need to be rubbing shoulders with him.

Tess tried not to glare when she looked at her friend across the room. When she glanced at Casey, she felt her expression soften.

He was wearing a black jersey under an oversized black jacket, and his faded jeans had a fashionable tear in the knee. A book bag sat on the floor at his feet. Some girls might not have found him handsome, but she wanted to walk over and run her hands through his long blond hair, hair that defied the school dress code, along with an earring in one lobe.

He wasn't a complete rebel because he excelled in most of his classes, but everybody knew Casey had a way of setting his own agenda, and she liked that.

S.W. didn't mind his style, either, and she seemed to have a dreamy look in her gray eyes as she watched Casey rise and pick up his satchel. S. W wasn't as trim as Tess, but she had a cute face, which she enhanced with bright red lipstick. Sometimes she got depressed about her looks, but her tangle of chestnut hair was like a mane that was hard to miss. Tess would have to refrain from pulling it out if S.W. was indeed trying to come on to Casey.

How could she be thinking about that kind of silliness now? Tess wanted to kick herself. They were here to consider things far more grave than petty jealousies.

She could worry about winning Casey's attention later, after they'd dealt with matters at hand.

Nervously, she turned to Charisse. "I had to get scented candles. That was all they had in black."

"That should be fine," Charisse said. She took the bag and picked out one of the candles. She sniffed at it and wrinkled her nose. "If it doesn't gag us."

"They said it was sandalwood."

"Yes, that's what it smells like. Well, this is all of us. Are we ready to begin?"

"As ready as we're going to get," Casey said. He was trying to appear calm, but Tess knew him well enough to detect some nervousness, although he'd probably deny it. At least he wasn't trembling quite as badly as Nathan.

Nathan was perpetually nervous, but he was even more fidgety than usual as he walked to the center of the room along with S.W. He was a thin guy, about a foot shorter than Casey, and he wore sandy hair cropped short on the sides and combed with a neat part on top. He wore a simple blue shirt and jeans, and Tess could see his collar was almost flapping with his movement.

Inside she felt the same way. She drew in a long breath and then exhaled in an effort to calm herself. It would have been even nicer to take Casey's hand, but she couldn't do that, at least not spontaneously.

"Are we going to do this here?" Casey asked.

Charisse shook her head. "Downstairs. We have a basement."

"A-a-re we ready to start?" Nathan asked.

"That's why you wanted to come here wasn't it?" Charisse responded.

He nodded.

"You asked me if I could help you. I can, but I need your help as well."

"Let's get on with it, then," Tess said.

"What exactly are we going to do?" S.W. asked.

"We'll go over that as we go along," Charisse said softly. Her matter-of-fact tone rattled Tess.

She was weird, as weird as this house. They couldn't go along with this, they needed to run for the door. They needed to forget this whole crazy idea.

Except they'd come too far for that. Charisse had only hinted at what they might actually do to take care of Bran; and while they'd been able to imagine possibilities, those had been only daydreams.

Now they were about to take the final steps toward—did she even dare imagine it—black magic.

Slowly, they followed Charisse, the hardwood floor creaking under their weight as they headed out of the parlor and through a larger living area and an old kitchen.

Beside the refrigerator a doorway led downward, down a rickety flight of stairs and into darkness. Charisse flicked on a light switch, and a bare white bulb flared to life.

The basement was almost empty except for a few boxes stacked against one wall, but with the shadows cast by the bulb, the room seemed ominous. The floor was black and smooth, as if it had been prepared not as the simple floor of a storage room but instead as a functional area.

"You have to help me get ready," Charisse said.

11

"Do we have to put on robes or anything?" Nathan asked. "No, nothing as theatrical as that." She handed the candles to Casey. "Hold these a moment."

She moved over to the boxes and pulled out a container of white chalk. Selecting a piece, she walked back to the center of the room, then gracefully lowered herself into a crouch. Quickly she set about sketching a five-pointed star with inter-connecting lines.

"Place the candles at the points," she instructed Casey when she had finished.

He split the candles with Nathan, and they began to put them down. S.W. moved close to Tess then.

"This is scary," she whispered.

Tess flashed a worried look back at her. She couldn't argue. Unless Charisse was just a little twisted and had decided to kid them, this was beginning to look serious.

While the boys were finishing with the candles, Charisse took a small hand bell from one of the boxes and again paced to the center of the room. Raising the bell, she began to ring it over her head in a circular motion, turning slowly as she did. The loud chimes echoed off the walls, almost deafening the group.

"What's that for?" S.W. asked.

"It's a purification," Charisse answered. She continued the ringing for almost a full minute before placing the bell on the floor outside the star.

"Did you bring the items I requested?" she asked.

Casey slung his bag off his shoulder and pulled the zipper back. From inside, he pulled a red-and-black plaid scarf. It was slightly worn looking, as if it had seen a couple of winters.

Tess recognized it as belonging to Bran. She'd seen it wrapped around his neck a few times and had dreamed of drawing it tighter.

"I got it off his chair in the cafeteria at lunch," Casey said.

"It should serve our needs," Charisse said. Taking the cloth, she wound it into a tight ball, which she then rolled between her hands. Her eyes closed as she began to concentrate.

"Yes, this will serve," she said. With her head, she motioned toward the star.

"Let us move into the pentagram," she said. "We will need its protection."

"From what?" Nathan asked.

"Inquisitive, aren't you?" she said. "What do you think?"

Nathan's face grew pale, and he wasted no time in moving into the area at the center of the drawing. The others moved there as well, and with Charisse's instructions, they were soon standing back to back.

"Light the candles," she said.

Casey pulled a pack of matches from his jeans and stepped forward. When he was finished, Charisse flipped off the light sw.

The room became a different place. The candles created a dance of shadows. An array of shapes shimmered around the room, and the light glowed ominously.

"Before we proceed, you have to decide what you want to do," Charisse said. "Do you wish to help yourselves, or do you wish to destroy Bran?"

"We don't want to hurt anyone," Tess said emphatically. "We just want him to leave us alone. We're tired of being terrorized."

Charisse nodded, her expression unchanging. "Did each of you do as I asked?"

They all nodded.

"Very well."

She went over to the boxes again, and when she returned this time, she carried what appeared to be a small metal bowl. "Let's get started."

She stepped into the symbol and placed the bowl on the floor. "Join me in the calling," she said.

Tess could hear the rain somewhere outside, somewhere that seemed very far away. The basement had become like a cavern deep within the earth. She realized that the small windows, which might normally have let in light, had been painted black.

A roar of thunder sounded suddenly, making her jump, but Charisse ignored it. Positioning everyone in the back-to-back circle again, she began a low chant, her voice rising, forming words that could not be understood.

The thunder sounded again, and then the rain seemed to fall harder, beating against the covered windows, hammering at the glass.

13

Tess held her breath. This was a game to Charisse. It had to be. She was making a big joke of all of them. They'd been so desperate to get out from under Bran's reign of terror they'd been susceptible.

There was no way this was going to do any good, and when it was over, Charisse would probably wave goodbye and have a big laugh about it. It was probably her way of getting revenge because she hadn't been readily accepted into the social circles at Pembrook High.

"Did each of you do as I asked with your request?" Charisse asked when she had stopped chanting.

"Yes," they said in unison.

"Give them to me."

Each of the group members produced a piece of paper. Charisse had instructed them to put into writing what they wanted the spell to achieve. They were supposed to keep it a secret.

Tess had scribbled down that she wanted only to be free of any more of Bran's retribution. She didn't want biblical plagues or anything. All she wanted was peace.

She wondered what the others had written, but it didn't really matter, she reminded herself. Nothing was going to happen.

Charisse collected the papers and turned with the bowl in front of her. From somewhere in the folds of her dress, she produced a sharp little stiletto.

"I need blood," she said.

Tess opened her eyes wide, and she heard S.W. gasp at the suggestion.

"Just a touch," Charisse said.

Gently she took Tess's wrist and touched the blade point to Tess's fingertip. Then she squeezed until a crimson drop oozed out and spilled into the bowl on top of the slips of paper. Charisse repeated the process with each of the others, and when she was finished, she took Casey's matches and lit one.

Dropping the flame into the bowl, she sat it down again and watched it blaze bright orange for a moment.

As the blaze slowly died, she whispered another series of unintelligible words, moaning until the flame was completely gone.

Her hand plunged into the bowl, and she grabbed a handful of the black ashes then, crumbling them and casting them into the air.

The charred fragments floated slowly back to the floor, and she picked up the bell again, ringing it in similar fashion.

The noise was louder than the storm as it bounced off the corners of the room, a harsh peal that sounded like pain.

Three

Forces of Midnight

"You think it'll have any effect?" Tess asked later as the four of them sat around a table at The Petite Burger, Pembrook's most famous hamburger restaurant.

Casey dabbed a French fry into a blob of ketchup, swirling it. "It was an interesting experiment, but I don't know what to expect. I don't think I really believe in magic. If anything happens, it'll be because we all focused our concentration, not because we have any supernatural forces in play."

"I don't think I follow you," Nathan said.

"Negative energy," Casey said. "If we generated enough of it, that might make Bran leave us alone. Otherwise, it'll be business as usual."

"If we generated psychic energy, isn't that magic?" S.W. asked.

"No. It's not even supernatural," Casey said. "It could just be that you're thinking about something really hard, so you give off subtle subconscious clues. Somebody else's subconscious picks up on it, and they react to it. Not magic at all. Not really even psychic. Just human nature."

"So you don't believe in magic?" Tess asked. Her hamburger was uneaten on her plate. She hadn't had an appetite since the ceremony.

Casey looked toward the window where the rain was splattering against the glass. The wind had also picked up, and the clouds were almost black.

"I'm not sure. I'm curious about everything. I just don't know of much evidence that proves magic is real, or that it works beyond a subconscious level."

"Charisse seemed to know what she was doing," Nathan said.

That made Casey smirk. "She's probably read a few paperback spell books. What I think about her is that she's a new girl who's kind of lonely, and when we asked her what she could do, she figured it was a good way to get attention."

"Why'd you bother then?" Tess asked.

"I didn't decide that until I saw her work," he said. "I'd have to have a look."

Tess bowed her head. "I kind of wish we hadn't gone through with it."

"Why?" S.W. asked. "It might get Bran off our backs, even if it is because we're giving him negative subconscious signals—which, I have to say, I don't think would work on Bran Hatten."

"I feel guilty, if you want the truth," Tess said. "Sure he's mean, but whether or not it's real, we were in that basement trying to conjure bad things for him."

"Not bad things," Casey said. "I don't know about the rest of you, but I just wrote that I wanted him to lighten up."

"I just said I wanted to be left alone," Nathan offered. "I didn't wish anything bad on him."

S.W. shrugged. "Me, either. Nothing really bad."

Tess twisted a lock of her hair around her finger. "Why don't we just forget about it?"

"That sounds good to me," S.W. said. "We won't see him before Monday anyway, and we're not going to have much time to think about him. I'm going to my grandmother's for Thanksgiving."

"We have company coming to our house," Nathan said. Casey lifted his hands, palms up, gesturing toward the others. "See, nothing to it. We're forgetting already."

Tess pushed her plate away from her. "I hope you're right."

"Relax," he said.

Getting up from the table, they headed for the door en masse; but once outside, S.W., Nathan, and Casey headed for The Judge, leaving Tess to drive home alone.

She didn't like driving in the rain, but she didn't have much choice. She gave them a brief flutter of a wave, and then darted from under the restaurant's eaves.

The cold November rain bit at Tess, until she made it to her car. She quickly fired the engine to life, then started the heater and her windshield wipers.

Maybe the bleak weather was spooking her. Maybe that was the reason she felt so strange. She had no reason to believe their little endeavor had stirred up any evil forces.

She had other things to think about besides Bran, anyway. Even though the holidays were on, she was supposed to be using the time to get a jump on her term paper about Macbeth. While the play contained witches, she couldn't really count this afternoon's activities as research.

Shoving the gearshift into reverse, she eased the long car out of the parking slot and pulled slowly onto Montgomery Street which led back into the residential section where Tess lived.

She didn't have the feeling that she was being followed until she'd traveled a couple of blocks, but then, instantly, the sensation settled over her. The thin hairs on the back of her neck stood on end, and a tingle spread down her back and across her shoulders.

She looked quickly in the rearview, but no ominous black sedans were in pursuit, and no horned creatures with leathery wings were baring down on her.

Too much imagination, she decided, and turned on the radio. A blast of music should help, she thought, but instead she got only static through the speakers—dry, hissing static, punctuated by additional crackles as lightning streaked the sky in the distance. Reaching over, she twisted the tuning knob to find a station, but the static continued.

When the voice sounded, it was so abrupt that she almost jumped back in the seat. She had to remind herself to keep steering. At first, she thought she was hearing an ad, but then she realized the deep tone was not some radio announcer. It was more unearthly.

Beware the forces of midnight lest you be devoured.

18

Even with both hands on the wheel, she almost lost control. She felt the car veering and had to slam on the brakes. On the wet pavement, the tires did not immediately grip. They slid across the wet film that covered the road, and the car slalomed, pitching from side to side. Tess fought the wheel, trying to get the vehicle under control.

Nothing seemed to work, as if something had taken control. She knew it was only the slick road and the heavy car's momentum, but she couldn't shake the idea that some an otherworldy force was present.

Screaming, she gripped the wheel even tighter, trying to remember instructions from driver's ed. Steer with the skid, they'd said. As the car continued to slide, twisting about in the roadway, she tried to obey the rules, letting the wheel go as it wanted. Panic was trying to seize her, but she bit her lip and willed her arms to relax slightly.

The car leaned to one side, and the body seemed to bounce on the frame, but she kept calm, kept guiding the wheel. The spin had almost completed a circle, and some of the force was slowing. She applied the brake a little more gradually, and the car continued to slow down.

It came to a stop just before jumping the curb on the left-hand side of the street. She was lucky she had not met any oncoming traffic or a collision would have been inevitable.

She leaned her head back against the headrest and sighed with relief. What a crazy afternoon. She'd let it all get to her and had almost crashed the car. She would have been grounded until she was on Social Security if that had happened.

But it hadn't. No harm done, and nothing to be worried about. She started to pull away from the curb when she heard the crackle of static again.

No words came through the speakers this time, however, only a deep, frightening sound of …laughter.

Four

Bran

Bran Hatten stepped out of the drugstore and turned up the collar of his worn fatigue jacket against the rain. He'd inherited the coat from his old man, who'd worn it on a peace time tour of duty that had included Guam and later Fort Polk, Louisiana.

It wasn't exactly a meaningful memento, but it was all he had. That was only part of the reason he hung on to it, however. He didn't remember much about his pop. He had split when Bran had been just a kid, so he wasn't particularly sentimental.

He liked the jacket more because it gave him a tough look. Coupled with his almost shaved head, the hint of a military demeanor scared more than a few people out of his way. Bran had discovered a long time ago that 90 percent of the people he encountered could be intimidated just by his look.

They wanted to go about their business. They didn't want to be troubled by confrontation. When they saw him coming at school, a lot of the wimps ducked their heads and moved quickly along, trying to avoid him.

Sometimes those signs of submission were enough. Other times he decided to push things a little further, proving that getting out of his way was a good idea. It reminded other kids he was not to be bothered, and it confirmed for him that he was formidable.

He had come downtown this afternoon to look at magazines. Even on a holiday week the new periodicals were distributed by mid-week, and he'd wanted to check out the latest copy of *Wheels*. It had arrived, and he'd walked out with a copy tucked inside his coat.

One of these days he'd get a job and buy himself a car to fix up. He'd do it just like those in the magazines, and then he'd get out of this crappy little town and away from everything.

At the corner the light was just changing, but he stepped on the street anyway, walking slowly. A station wagon was just about to pull forward, but the driver had to wait. Bran turned his head and glared at her as he ambled along, making no effort to hurry.

He was planning to head straight home and thumb the magazine when he spotted Hammond Easterman a couple of blocks ahead. Hammond was a tall guy who'd probably become an English major one day.

Everyone thought he was nice, but Bran couldn't look at him without seething. Hammond always knew the answers in class. The bastard. He'd caused Bran to be laughed at once.

He'd apparently been doing some Christmas shopping this afternoon. He was carrying a plastic shopping bag from Clementine's Bookshop. Of course, a dweeb would think books made a good gift.

He was moving at a light jog, holding his white wind-breaker closed over his shirt. Since his head was ducked against the rain, he didn't notice Bran. He probably would have crossed to the other side of the street if that had been the case.

That was his bad luck, Bran thought. Quickening his pace, he moved forward, stopping in the center of the sidewalk about half a block away from Hammond.

The dweeb almost didn't notice him, but he stopped just short of colliding with Bran and started to move to the side to keep going. Then his eyes focused on just who it was in his path.

He stopped abruptly and looked at Bran, his eyes bulging behind the glasses he wore.

Hammond was a tall guy but skinny, and his neat blond hair, which he wore swept back from his forehead, made him look like he was already a professor as far as Bran was concerned.

"Taking home some light reading, Hammond?"

"Getting in some early Christmas shopping," he said nervously.

"Thought so."

21

In a quick motion, he grabbed for the bag in Hammond's hand. Before the boy could react, the bag was in Bran's possession. It was a bright yellow sack with a draw string closure at the top.

Bran tugged it open and looked inside. "Got some intellectual reading?" he asked.

"Just some gifts."

Bran reached inside and pulled out a large blue paperback.

He squinted as he scanned the cover. It was written by some guy with a Mexican name: *One Hundred Years of Solitude*. "What's this about?"

"It's hard to explain. It's a story with what's called magic realism."

"Yeah, okay. That kind of crap."

He let the book slide from his fingers, and it slapped to the wet sidewalk.

Hammond started to pick it up, but Bran slammed his foot down on the book cover, twisting his heavy boot from side to side until grime smeared across the cover and the pages began to tear.

"Come on," Hammond protested. "That was expensive."

"Sorry."

He grabbed the book sack by the bottom and tilted it, letting all of the books and cards inside spill out.

Hammond shouted and started to gather them up, but Bran leered at him, letting him know he'd be dead meat if he gave it a try. Hammond stopped, his lips trembling as he watched the drizzle fall onto his purchases, ruining them.

He wasn't crying, but he wanted to, Bran decided. That brought a grin to the bully's face. Hammond knew who was in charge.

"Sorry," Bran said, broadening his grin.

Hammond looked at him hard. He wanted to pick up his stuff, but he knew he couldn't.

"Did you say something?" Bran asked.

"You sure?"

Bran edged forward. In the rain there weren't many people out and about, so he wasn't worried about being disturbed. If someone did happen along, he'd just deny there were any problems, but for the moment, he had time to kill.

"What's the matter, Hammond? You mad about your books?" Hammond didn't speak. He just stood there, water starting to bead on his glasses.

"Guess you didn't get that jump on your Christmas shopping after all, eh? Bad luck."

He flexed his fingers. He could give the kid a good punch right here. He could take him off his feet if he wanted, and that would be a good laugh, watching the class genius sit there on the sidewalk with a bloody lip.

Slowly, he began to raise his arm, the muscles tensing. Good night, pretty boy.

Before he could swing, something weird seized him. He stopped in mid-motion as an odd chill moved over him. For a second he thought a cold burst of wind had swept around the corner, but then he realized that the sensation was not external.

It was coming from inside him.

That rattled him. Had he suddenly been struck sick? He stepped back from Hammond and looked around, trying to figure out what was suddenly going on.

It didn't make sense, and he shook his head, trying to clear his thoughts. He was shuddering for no reason. It was cold, but not that cold, especially not with him wearing his coat.

Hammond looked at him, perplexed. Bran wanted to hit Hammond, wanted to knock him off his feet, but he couldn't bring himself to make the move. He didn't feel right.

Without speaking further, Bran turned and hurried back up the street, then rounded the corner and moved on, not running but not wasting time.

He was frightened, frightened in a way he'd never been before. He couldn't really decide what had scared him. He only wanted to get home, get to his room … somewhere safe.

Five

Back to School

Tess found herself dreading school more than usual on the Monday after Thanksgiving. Parking in the student lot, she picked up her book satchel and hurried into the east wing. She had taken the trouble to pick out a crisp blue blouse and nice jeans that morning, but she thought her hair was too wild. She tried to smooth it with one hand as she entered the building.

Picking her way through the crowd, she searched for Casey. She hadn't talked to him since the ceremony because she'd been away at her grandmother's. The family had just rolled back into town Sunday night, so she'd had no chance to check with anyone, not even S.W.

Usually, Casey hung out in the chemistry lab before school. He didn't have any particular affinity for chemistry, but he had a couple of friends who were good with test tubes.

When she stopped by there, however, she found only a couple of guys in white lab coats who were already busy firing up Bunsen burners and checking petri dishes.

Her uneasy feeling seemed to deepen. The foreboding that had developed after the car incident had continued to hang over her throughout the holiday, and now it seemed even worse.

Maybe nothing was wrong; maybe the warning had been her imagination, but she couldn't shake a feeling that something stranger than they had hoped for was occurring.

Finally she located Casey at his locker. He was wearing a white shirt and black vest with a slightly better pair of jeans than usual.

"What's happening?" he asked.

24

She leaned against the locker beside him. He looked cuter than ever with his hair pulled back in a ponytail.

"I was wondering how everything was going," she said.

"Fine." He gave her a warm smile. She wished all she had to worry about was whether or not he liked her.

"I've been out of town," she said. "Has anything weird happened?"

"You didn't hear?"

"What?"

"All hell broke loose. The gym exploded, stones fell from the sky. It was like Armageddon." He chuckled, and she swatted his arm.

"Seriously."

"Seriously," he said. "Nothing happened. All the rumors about Charisse were obviously just gossip, and all that mumbo jumbo we went through was just her idea of trying to get friends."

"Have you seen Bran?"

"What's a matter? You afraid he turned into a toad over the weekend?"

"Well…"

"Relax. He's fine. I saw him on front hall a few minutes ago shaking down some freshmen for their lunch money."

Tess closed her eyes and sighed with relief. She wasn't happy that he was bothering kids, but she was happy things seemed to be normal.

"Just forget about it," Casey said. "We had a fun little séance or whatever and it's over. Nothing's changed. We'll just stay out of Bran's way like we always have."

"Right," Tess said. "I can't say I'm happy about that, but it's better than having anything evil on my conscience."

"Where's S.W.?" he asked.

"I haven't seen her yet." She looked over at him. His question seemed to ne just an offhanded remark. He was probably just making conversation, but she didn't like the sound of the question.

If Bran wasn't in trouble she could concentrate on other business. What if Casey was interested in S.W. instead of her? She couldn't blame him. S.W. was always bubbly and laughing, and Tess always felt so serious.

She tried to think of a joke as they walked toward their first class, but she hadn't come up with anything by the time they reached the door.

S.W. was already there and looking far better than Tess would have liked. Her hair was a tangle of curls, but they were better arranged than Tess's. And she was wearing a great new sweater.

She smiled when she saw them.

"How's it going?" she asked.

"Okay," Casey said. "You didn't grow cloven hooves or anything, did you?"

"Not yet." She giggled as only S.W. could with a little twist in her throat.

They took their seats near a rear corner and opened their books. First hour was Algebra II, not something that Tess enjoyed, though she'd been told she'd need it for college.

The teacher for the class was Joseph Mooney, a man whose name was the source of endless jokes among the student body. He didn't laugh at any of them. He was a thin, humorless man who wore thick glasses.

Everyone fell silent when he entered and growled a good morning. The responses to his salutation were muffled at best, but he ignored those and quickly ran through the roll call.

"No welcome back or anything," Tess observed. "What'd he do? Spend his holiday in cold storage?"

"Probably in a morgue," S.W. whispered back.

Once the roll was finished, the class moved immediately into the discussion of a new set of problems. Mooney took a place at the podium and began to discuss the applications of several formulas.

After he'd gone over some examples, he nodded toward the class. "Now let's see if we can't work some of these things out at the board," he suggested.

"Miss Ryan, Mr. Sargent, Miss Tate, and Mr. Hatten, would you come forward please?"

With a roll of her eyes, Tess picked up her book, tucked her pencil between the pages and moved to the front of the classroom, where she took a spot at the blackboard. The other kids who'd been called joined her, but she was thankful Bran's spot was at the opposite end of the board.

While she waited for further instructions, she picked up a piece of yellow chalk and rolled it in her fingers. She didn't like being in front of the group, and she could feel all of the eyes locked on her, or at least they seemed to be.

Finally Mooney called out a page number, and she flipped to it. The equations there looked as odd as a foreign language. She had enough trouble puzzling through math problems without having to do them as performance art.

"Let's see if you can apply what we've learned," he said.

Facing the board, Tess rolled her eyes again. This was one of Mooney's tests to see how well the students listened. He would extol the virtues of those who'd caught on and make examples of those who hadn't.

Richey Sargent, who was probably going to become an electrical engineer upon graduation, would obviously excel up here, and Lucy Tate would fare okay also. Tess and Bran would be the test subjects, the ones who would probably have to have assistance.

"Mr. Hatten, take problem one," Mooney said. "Mr. Sargent, number two; Miss Tate, number three; and Miss Ryan, number four."

Great, Tess thought. Everyone would be foundering on their own. She titled her head down and began to write the equation on the board. The first step in solving a problem was writing it down, Mooney always said.

Once she had it in front of her, she began concentrating on making sense of the X's and Y's involved. She'd taken in enough of what Mooney had said to at least get started, so she quickly worked out the obvious portions.

She was so focused, she didn't pay any attention to the others working beside her. Mooney would probably have commented if anyone even glanced away from their own work.

The titters began to draw her attention a second later, however. She glanced back over her shoulder. Had she done something so obviously stupid that all of the students could detect the fallacy of her logic?

Their eyes didn't seem to be focused on her. They were looking more in Bran's direction. She turned her head, craning her neck to get a look at what he was writing.

It wouldn't be out of the question for him to be scribbling snide remarks instead of doing his problem.

At first, she thought he was just scrawling aimless words, but then she began to focus on the lines he was drawing.

"What's going on, Mr. Hatten?" Mooney asked.

Bran couldn't speak. He just kept making marks with his chalk. Tess took a step back, getting a better look at the lines. They weren't words, at least not in any language she recognized. Yet there seemed to be an order to what he was doing.

As Mooney moved toward the board, she snatched her pencil from her book and flipped back to the blank end plate. Hurriedly she began to scribble down the mysterious things Bran was writing.

Before she could get it all down, Mooney picked up an eraser and wiped the marks away.

"I know you have contempt for this class, Mr. Hatten," he said. "But some of the people are here to learn. It wouldn't hurt you to try instead of scribbling this meaningless drivel up here."

Bran stepped back, and his mouth dropped open. He seemed surprised, as if he didn't recognize the marks Mooney was now smearing into dust.

"I didn't mean to..."

"Just take your seat," Mooney said. "The rest of you can stop gawking and continue. Mr. Hatten and I will have a little talk after class."

Tess turned immediately back to the board, but she stared down at the odd scribblings. They gave her an uneasy feeling. Absently, she chewed at her finger.

Maybe Bran had just been playing his usual games, but he seemed genuinely perplexed. A new feeling of apprehension churned Tess's stomach. What if he'd been writing some sort of magical words, words he truly couldn't control?

After class, she caught up with Casey in the hallway.

"What did you make of that?"

"Nothing," he said.

"What was he writing?"

"It was Bran. He was just scribbling."

She put a hand on his arm and stopped him. "Are you sure?"

28

He thought for a moment, then shrugged. "Reasonably."

"Didn't the markings look kind of arcane to you?"

"Maybe."

"What if it is some kind of magic?"

"Then the spell worked, and he should leave us alone. It's obviously harmless."

"I don't know about that."

"It's a little weird. I'll grant you that, but I'm sure it's nothing to worry about."

"I hope you're right," Tess said.

The corners of Casey's lips turned up. "Forget it."

He walked on to his next class, and Tess turned also. She had to get moving, as well. Maybe there was nothing to worry about, but she couldn't be sure.

She'd have to find someone who might be able to identify what Bran had written, someone besides Charisse.

Six

Confusion

Bran felt confused as he left school that afternoon. His head had been reeling since first hour, and he couldn't understand what had happened at the chalk board. No matter how many times he searched his memory, he couldn't come up with an answer.

He'd thought he was copying the problem on the board, and he'd been as surprised as everyone else when he'd looked at the markings to discover some gibberish in front of him instead.

He didn't know any foreign languages even though he'd taken his required French course. He couldn't have written something in a foreign language if he'd wanted. That was what Mooney had accused him of doing, and the bum had assigned him an extra page of problems along with his homework, just what he needed.

His stepfather would have chores for him this evening. By the time he got around to homework, he'd be worn out, and to complete all the problems Mooney wanted he'd have to sit up until midnight. Unless he wanted to plant his butt in detention for an hour after school tomorrow. He had just a fine bunch of options.

If he hadn't been in a hurry to get home, he would have taken the situation out on someone, but he didn't have time to hunt for a victim. He just had to hope someone would happen by.

As he plodded along the sidewalk, he wondered if there was anything wrong with him. The odd chill had hit him the other day, and now he'd done something without realizing it. Was that some kind of warning sign?

He'd seen enough television shows where that sort of sign predicted the disease of the week. Raising a hand to his almost slick head as he walked, he let his fingers move over his skull. He found no cracks, but he wondered if he had a tumor nestled in there somewhere.

The old man had swatted his head enough times. If being conked could give you a tumor, Bran was as qualified as anyone. He'd been slapped around by his mother's second husband for as long as he could remember.

The old man seemed to resent Bran just because he was there, because he'd come along with his mother as part of the package. The old man didn't like having extra baggage, so whenever he'd had the chance over the years, he'd punished Bran.

Bran had survived for spite as much as anything, doing as he was told and enduring whatever the old man dished out without flinching. Had the old man found a way to win in the long run?

Couldn't be. He couldn't have caused a tumor. Bran pulled his hand down. Maybe it was some early winter flu. Whatever he had, he'd get over it.

With his hands deep in his pockets, he moved on along the sidewalk, ducking his head as a brisk November wind picked up.

He was thinking about taking a shortcut across a vacant lot when he spotted Nathan, also walking.

The little jerk had an aunt or something on Stevens Street, only a block from Bran's house. Bran saw him in the neighborhood frequently. Usually he ignored him, but today he had promised himself he'd deal with anybody he spotted.

Taking his hands out of his pockets, he picked up his pace, his heavy, black boots hammering the pavement as he moved. The sound alerted Nathan who was a half block away.

He looked back, and immediately a look of fear crossed his features. Bran had to smile. If Bran Hatten was coming toward you at a brisk pace, you knew you were in trouble. He liked that.

He watched Nathan's features twitch as he tried to decide what to do, but before the kid could make up his mind to run, Bran was there, joining him at the corner.

"What's up, Nat?" he asked with a grin.

31

"Nothing much," Nathan said nervously. He was carrying a couple of books, and he shifted them slightly.

Bran noticed the legs of his jeans vibrating. The kid was trembling, and his stomach was probably in knots. The expression was probably the expression the old man had seen on Bran's face a few times, at least in the early years, before Bran had learned to keep a stoic look to rob the old man of some of his pleasures.

"Whatcha doin' in the neighborhood?" he asked pleasantly.

"Just visiting," Nathan said. "I-I was going to see my Aunt Agnes."

"Isn't she a little crazy?"

"She's just old. Sometimes I do chores for her."

"What kind of chores?" Bran asked. He slid his fingers slowly around the back of Nathan's neck, tightening his grip gradually.

"Just taking out her trash, that kind of thing." He quivered even more as Bran's fingers began to bite into his neck. "That's not much fun for a cool guy like you."

Tears were forming in Nathan's eyes now. The pain couldn't be that bad, but he was scared.

"You ever fall down while you're working?" Bran asked.

He didn't give Nathan time to respond. He quickly swept his heavy boot around, hooking his toe behind Nathan's ankles.

When his feet came out from under him, Nathan dropped his books and for an instant, he fanned his arms futilely in midair. He looked like he was trying to do some ridiculous bird imitation, but then he went down, slamming onto the sidewalk.

The air rushed out of his lungs in an audible whoosh, and he lay almost still. Real sobs began to form in his throat as he lay there, uncertain of whether he should try to get up or brace himself for more punishment.

Bran stood over him for a second with his hands on his hips. From Nathan's viewpoint he probably looked like the Jolly Green Giant. He grinned down at the kid, beginning to laugh.

His snicker became a deep guffaw. "Looks like you lost your balance. I don't know if you could be much help to some poor little old lady."

He continued to grin as Nathan struggled into a sitting position. Bran realized he could stomp him there right now, could grind his heel down into the boy's ribs, or he could crush a hand.

The impulse to move his foot started to form, and the muscle even twitched slightly, but for some reason his limb did not respond as he wanted. The smile faded slowly from his face, and he looked down at his leg.

Nothing seemed to be wrong with it, but he couldn't make it respond. His foot seemed to be glued down to the concrete. Grunting, he tried to force it to move, but nothing happened. From the corner of his eye, he saw Nathan getting up. The punk had realized something was wrong. He was going to make a run for it, but that was a moot point. Bran didn't care about that now. He had other concerns.

Nathan pushed himself up off the concrete, and without bothering to pick up his books, bolted, running as fast as he could along the street toward his aunt's house.

Even if he could have, Bran would not have chased him. The fear he had generated, the fact that he could make the kid run that way was satisfying, but he couldn't enjoy his accomplishment.

Not at the moment.

Bending down, he wrapped his hands around his leg and began to massage the muscles. There didn't seem to be any numbness. He wasn't having a muscle spasm.

Something else had to be wrong. He felt the fear begin as a sudden burst in the pit of his stomach, and then it crawled up through his abdomen, into his chest.

If he had a brain tumor, wouldn't it prevent messages from his brain to travel properly to the rest of his body?

The fear was terrible as he considered that. Was this just the beginning? Were things going to get worse?

He'd had a chill, written gibberish on a chalk board, and now he had a frozen limb. What was next? Was he going to wind up some blithering, mindless idiot?

Please, not that. He didn't like things that were beyond his control.

As he struggled to move his leg, he let out a loud yell of anger.

Seven

Strangers

Word travelled fast about Bran's experience at the blackboard. Most people figured it was just another of his acts of rebellion, but others speculated that he might be losing it—big time!

Anyone who'd ever suffered under Bran's reign of terror enjoyed the latter notion. At lunch, kids chuckled and joked and tapped their temples, indicating his lunacy.

At lunch, Tess joined S.W, and, as they made their way through the cafeteria line, they discussed the incident just as the kids in front of them were doing.

"Can you believe it?" asked one girl. "He's always been weird, but this time he's gone bonkers."

Her companion giggled.

"I think it's a little more serious than they realize," Tess said.

"Maybe not," S.W. whispered with a shake of her head. "It could be something he thought of on the spur of the moment. Let's get a table."

Together, they made their way through the crowded room. It was a broad, open hall, and the chatter of voices echoed off the concrete block walls. Tess would've preferred a more quiet place to eat, but then she didn't have a choice.

Finally, she and S.W. selected a place near the window and began to survey their food. Pizza was the main item on today's menu, but that wasn't cause for celebration. It had the greasy regurgitated look of school cafeteria pizza rather than the creamy look of a more desirable pizza restaurant pie.

"Delicious," Tess said sarcastically as she took a bite. She placed the slice back on her tray. "This looks like that thing in that *Star Trek* episode. You remember?"

Tess was about to bring up Bran, but a voice sounded behind her.

"Mind if I join you guys?"

She turned to see Charisse standing with tray in hand. She wasn't smiling, but her expression seemed bright.

"Care if I sit down?" she asked.

"Sure," S.W. said before Tess could think of some polite way to decline.

Charisse wasted no time in settling into a chair. She looked great with her long, red hair brushed smooth and full. It was as beautiful as satin. Suddenly Tess felt chunky and unattractive in Charisse's presence—she was so lovely and exotic looking!

"What's going on?" Charisse asked as she opened her milk carton and stuck in her straw.

"Another lovely day at Pembrook High," S.W. said.

"Tell me about it."

"Did you hear about Bran?" Tess asked.

Charisse pushed a lock of her hair back and picked up her pizza. "No. What'd he do?"

"He wrote weird stuff on the blackboard."

"Wow."

"Do you think that had anything to do with our spells?" The words just spilled out before Tess could stop them. S.W. kicked her under the table, but Charisse didn't seem fazed.

She took a bite of pizza, then wrinkled her brow. "Did you will it? It requires concentrated will."

"Well, with all the rumors about you ... I mean, you know, stories that started from the minute you showed up. That's why we came to you. I mean, Bran wasn't bothering you like other girls, and you are pretty. We believed you were... you know."

Charisse smiled. "Then you did will it?"

"I don't know," Tess said.

"Don't let your imagination run away with you. I didn't ask for the rumors," Charisse said.

Tess waited for more of an explanation, but Charisse didn't provide one. She was more interested in pizza than confirming or denying whether rumors were true or whether she was just playing mind games.

After lunch, Tess and S.W. hurried toward gym class, leaving Charisse alone. She watched them go almost reluctantly. They seemed so suspicious.

People were always suspicious, everywhere, but Charisse had hoped they would warm to her if she helped them or seemed to help them. Maybe the ceremony had been a mistake. Maybe she shouldn't have allowed any hint of black magic or darkness. Now they thought she was weird.

Was she? She'd made an effort when she'd arrived to act as normal as possible, but there was something about her, something indefinable, an aura of the mysterious, which she couldn't get rid of. It was due in part to her gazes—which were sometimes too intense—and her frequent silences. She had to work on that. She had to learn to make conversation and keep things light.

She wanted the kids to be comfortable with her, to like her, to trust her.

Instead they were as hesitant as they had been when they'd first approached her—if not more so. If she wasn't careful, they'd be putting out a whole new string of rumors to go with the ones that had developed because she lived in an old house and kept quiet and to herself.

She'd have to keep working on them. One of the reasons she'd come here, back to Pembrook, was to combat the loneliness. She was tired of the feeling of isolation, tired of the empty feeling that came with the lack of community and friendship.

It was time for a change, and she could win people around. She knew she could. Things could be different for her. She would make sure things were different. She'd learned how to look out for herself.

She moved along the hallway which ran across the back of the school, and she watched the faces of those who passed. So many of them were strangers, and they didn't notice her or welcome her.

At least indifference was better than hostility.

She reached her locker and slowly began to spin the knob on her combination lock. As it dropped open, she shoved her books from the morning classes inside.

Several candles and an amulet were tucked in the bottom as well as an old yearbook photo of Bran. She moved those aside before selecting her books for the afternoon.

Eight

The Mad Hat Excursion

Tess and S.W. decided a trip to the mall was in order after school. With the anxiety Bran was generating, they needed to get rid of some stress.

They took the Buick and luckily found an empty slot near the main entrance.

"Somebody was nice enough to go home early," Tess said, angling the car carefully into the narrow space.

"Or this space is radioactive," S.W. quipped as she grabbed for her purse, and the two climbed out.

Giggling in a way they had not enjoyed for a while, they walked toward the mall's high-arched entranceway, which looked like the passage into some vast palace.

Inside they found a grand display of Christmas decorations already filling the massive hallway. Mechanical animals and elves were at work with jerky robotic motions in a fenced off display.

"It's Christmas time," S.W. said, waving to one of the green-clad elves, who seemed to be shaking a wooden mallet. "Really captures the spirit of the season doesn't?"

"Oh, I don't know," Tess said. "I think they're kind of cute." In spite of complaints about the commercialism, she always felt a rush of adrenalin as the Christmas season got underway.

"Who should we shop for?" she asked as they moved past the display and along the wide row of shops, where massive wreaths and candy canes were attached above the storefronts.

"Ourselves," S.W. said. "I hear Samantha's has a sale on hats."

Slowly, they began to make their way through the crowd. People were rushing everywhere, and most of the shoppers already had their arms filled with shopping bags and gift-wrapped packages.

"Shouldn't we start thinking about gifts?" Tess protested. "I haven't even started looking for things for my family."

"The way you've been moping around? No way! We're going to get something to perk you up."

"I don't have that much money, and I've got a lot of gifts to buy."

"You've got baby-sitting money, and your allowance. You're loaded."

They pushed on, elbowing and dodging and ignoring some cat calls from a group of guys wearing Hancock High lettermen jackets.

"They were cute," S.W. admitted.

"Yeah, but they could learn better ways of approaching us."

"We're so hot they couldn't control themselves," suggested S.W.

"Right."

"It's true. At least with you."

Tess blushed. "Stop it."

They were passing a lingerie store, and S.W. turned and nodded toward a lacy, rose-colored camisole displayed on a mannequin. "And that would look great on you. Especially with your hair."

"No way!" Tess said, turning her head with an exaggerated but embarrassed grin.

"It would get Casey's attention," S.W. chided.

"I don't think I'm ready for that much attention."

Tess kept walking, but S.W. stayed in front of the showcase for a moment, smiling as she looked over the selection.

Stepping back, Tess grabbed her arm and tugged her along. "Come on. I'll let you twist my arm about the hats."

Samantha's was a small locally-owned accessories shop sandwiched between larger dress shops. Sale signs filled the windows, which were arrayed with an assortment of scarves, jewelry, belts, and—of course, hats.

As they stepped into the shop, they headed straight for the corner where hats of all shapes and sizes were displayed and a small, square mirror was set up to accommodate customers who wanted to try them on.

Tess couldn't resist picking one up. It was a dark brown Fedora—the kind of hat Indiana Jones wore, or the kind Humphrey Bogart always had on in the movies her mom liked to watch.

She plopped it on her head, quickly pushing her hair back as she tilted the brim down over her forehead.

She pursed her lips when she looked into the mirror. The hat gave her a sinister, seductive look. She never thought of herself as sexy, but just for a moment, bolstered by the earlier hoots from the Hancock guys, she could imagine herself turning a few heads.

"Whoo, you look great," S.W. said, looking over her shoulder. "That's the one."

"I don't know," Tess said. She returned the hat to the rack. "Try this one," S.W. said, offering a blue hat with a floppy brim.

"Don't you think that's a little too goofy?" Tess asked.

"Try it."

She pulled the hat on and glanced into the mirror. It was a bit too wild looking, a little too much like something the Mad Hatter might wear.

"Not this one," she said.

"Okay, we'll try something else," S.W. said, returning the hat to the rack. She was about to pluck another, but Tess stopped her. She saw the one she wanted. It was a bright red hat with as round, turned up brim and a wide, black band.

"This is a little safer," she said.

Lowering it onto her crown, she glanced into the mirror. It didn't make her quite as alluring, but it went well with her hair and seemed to accent her smooth features. It would look great, especially if she wore bright red lipstick.

It might also help get Casey to notice her without sending too strong a signal. That was more what she wanted—a subtle enhancement.

"That looks terrific," the salesclerk said as she approached. She'd been busy with other customers but had now worked her way to them. She was about nineteen with curly blond hair, and she wore a tight black dress with a name tag that read Jenny.

"You look gorgeous in that," she said, taking Tess's shoulders and angling her back toward the mirror. "With some red earrings you'd knock 'em dead."

Tess smiled. "Earring aren't in the budget, but I might be able to swing the hat."

"You sure? I've got some great earrings on sale, too."

"Just the hat," Tess said. "I'll take it before you start talking belts."

"Maybe a belt would be good," S.W. said.

"Don't you start, too," Tess warned.

Reaching into her purse, she pulled out her wallet and followed Jenny over to the counter. As she rang up the price, a couple of other customers drifted in.

S.W. recognized the girls and began to talk to them, and that left Tess to wander around the store for a few more seconds after she'd paid the bill.

She found herself looking at earrings in spite of her intentions. Maybe some red ones would look good with the hat, she thought. She could try them on. She didn't have to buy them right now. Looking over the selection, she chose a pair of red, button-like clip-ons. She had pierced ears for several years now, but none of the pierced earrings were quite what she wanted.

These, on the other hand, were perfect. Clipping them to her lobes, she stepped in front of the mirror set into the wall, then slipped her hat from the bag to get an idea of the combo.

The earrings did look nice with the hat, and, for a moment, she contemplated whether or not she should drop some more cash here.

As she calculated her money holdings, her gaze wandered. The mirror was angled so that she could see the flow of the crowd behind her, and she began to watch the people move past.

There was quite an assortment. She saw a cluster of girls in plaid skirts from the parochial school across town; some elderly women; some housewives; and a couple of junior high boys, wearing baggy pants and jerseys.

She was still watching a moment later when she saw the parochial schoolgirls part suddenly. Wondering what had startled them, she turned and spotted Bran.

He was stomping along, head bowed, hands thrust deep into the pockets of his fatigue jacket. He seemed oblivious to everything around him; and, while she couldn't see him that well from a distance, his features seemed to be twisted into an angry scowl.

She felt a new flutter of anxiety. Maybe it was a troubled look. That couldn't be good.

"What's with Bran?" S.W. asked, approaching her from behind.

"I don't know."

Tess plucked off the earrings and returned them to their card. "Guess I don't really need these."

She reached for her hat, preparing to return it to the bag.

"Keep it on," S.W. suggested. "It's cute."

"If you say so." She took S.W.'s hand and gave it a quick squeeze. "Thanks for being a good friend."

"My pleasure."

"You're finished looking around?"

"Yeah, let's go get some yogurt parfaits."

"I don't know if that's what I want."

"Let's indulge. We're here to have fun."

"What if we run into Bran?"

"The last thing we want to do is let Bran ruin our fun. Come on."

Tess let S.W. take her arm, not resisting as she tugged her out of the store and back into the crowd. She looked around but caught no sight of Bran as they moved.

The yogurt shop was near one of the mall's fountains, a tower of silver blocks with a constant stream flowing down between them to a pool at the bottom.

While S.W. ordered, Tess watched the cascade, glistening in the sunbeams which filtered down through the skylight above.

She didn't notice Bran until her gaze happened to drift downward, and then she realized he was on the far side of the fountain. He too was staring into the water, but he didn't seem to be admiring the beauty. His gaze was transfixed, as if he was somehow mesmerized by the sight in front of him.

"S.W." Tess whispered.

S.W. turned, holding a sundae that was a couple of inches high and sprinkled with a rainbow-colored array of candies. "What?"

"Look at Bran."

"He's just looking at the fountain." She shoveled a mouthful of yogurt into her mouth.

"He's not just watching. He's hypnotized."

"Is he?" S.W. took another bite.

"Yes," Tess said.

They stepped away from the counter, still watching him. "He's always been kind of weird," S.W. said.

She continued to eat her yogurt as they moved a little closer to the fountain, watching Bran through the water. He still had his hands in his pockets, and his brow was wrinkled into his usual scowl.

"He's his usual cheerful self," S.W. said.

"He's worse than usual," Tess argued.

A second later he moved, confirming her contention. Without taking his hands from his pockets, he lifted one foot, moving it over the edge of the fountain pool.

"What's he doing?" S.W. asked.

"I don't know," Tess said, but her eyes opened wide.

He was climbing into the pool. Slowly, he eased his other foot over, and he began to wade through the knee-deep water. His expression didn't change, but he made his way to the fountain, and then he stood there, the cascading water splashing down over his head.

"I have to give you this," S.W. said as a crowd began to form and people began to laugh. "That doesn't look like something he'd come up with on his own."

"No," Tess agreed. "Someone must have suggested it to him, one way or another."

Nine

Night Walking

They met at Casey's that night.

As soon as Tess had made it home from the mall, she had called him, blurting what she'd seen. He'd agreed they needed to talk things over.

After supper, Tess picked up S.W. and they drove over to Casey's, parking behind The Judge in his driveway. They found Nathan and Casey in the family game room busy with a Nintendo.

Casey shut it off and showed the girls to seats on an old couch, which had been retired from the living room. It sagged slightly, and as she sat down Tess had a brief feeling of being swallowed.

"So he went wading," Casey said.

"In his combat boots," S.W. said.

"Nathan ran into Bran this afternoon, too," Casey said. "You want to tell them about it?"

Nathan nodded, and then briefly outlined what had happened to him on the sidewalk.

"He's definitely exhibiting strange behavior," Nathan concluded.

"I guess the question that concerns all of us is whether or not we're to blame," Casey observed.

He dropped into a chair and leaned back, propping his head against his hands. He wore dark, baggy slacks tonight and a loose-fitting red shirt with a dark vest, which featured a pattern of exotic postcards. He'd probably put his outfit together without much consideration, and Tess liked his nonchalant style.

"The fact remains that Bran was given to somewhat erratic behavior before we tried to put a spell on him," Casey said. "Did he do anything that out of the ordinary today? I mean out of the ordinary for Bran. From the chalkboard forward, his behavior has been only a slight exaggeration of what he usually does."

"He might have decided to step into the fountain pool any time," S.W. agreed. "Remember when he went tromping across the gym bleachers just after they were painted?"

"Or the time he jumped off the roof onto Mrs. Converse's convertible?" Casey added.

"But did he have a weird expression," Tess said.

"And something made him lay off me," Nathan said.

"Maybe he got a *hankerin'* to go walk in the mall fountain," Casey observed. "Seriously, if the spell were working he'd have left Nathan alone altogether wouldn't he?"

"Maybe whatever happened was the spell's way of making him leave Nathan alone," Tess said. "Besides, those markings on the board were like symbols."

Casey shook his head. "It's still hard to believe we really performed magic, with or without Charisse's help."

"But it's getting kind of scary," Nathan said.

"Maybe we're just letting it scare us," Casey suggested. "So what do we do?" Tess asked.

Casey shrugged. "The only thing we really can do right now is keep an eye on Bran, see what he does next."

"We need to check out Charisse, too," Tess suggested. "I mean, you know, watch her the same way."

"That should be enough at this point," Casey said. "After all, we don't have anything that earth shattering taking place. We just have active imaginations."

Tess wanted to believe him. She didn't like having her stomach twisted into a half-hitch, and she told herself what Casey was saying made plenty of sense.

Taking a deep breath, she held it for a second, then expelled it slowly, willing her system to purge all of her anxiety. The technique was fairly effective.

45

She settled back on the couch and crossed her legs, wondering if Casey had noticed her new hat. That was the sort of thing she was supposed to be wondering about, after all. Not about weird magic.

He did seem to be looking her way. She managed a smile and realized S.W. was observing the proceedings. For a moment, she thought she was going to be chided, but instead S.W. nodded toward Nathan.

"Was that a new game you were playing?" she asked. "Fairly new," Nathan said. "It's called Zombie Attack."

"Oh."

Tess knew S.W. was about as interested as mud in a game called *Zombie Attack*, but nonetheless S.W. let Nathan lead her over to the television where the game was set up. That left Tess alone with Casey. She was going to owe S.W. big time, but maybe it would be worth it.

Leaning forward slightly to escape the sinkhole at the center of the couch, she tried to think of something to say.

Casey saved her the trouble. "You want a Coke while they're busy with that?"

She hesitated a second, then gave him a nod.

"We're getting Cokes from the kitchen," he said. "You guys want anything?"

"Not now, thanks," Nathan said. He was already engrossed in the game.

"No thanks," S.W. said.

With a shrug, Casey led the way through the swinging door, which opened into the family's kitchen. After he'd pulled a couple of cans from the refrigerator, they sat on stools at the kitchen counter where Christmas decorations had been set out.

"I really don't think we have anything to worry about," he said. "As long as Bran's harassing people and vandalizing fountains, I don't think he's too bothered by any evil spirits we might have sicced on him."

"I hope you're right," Tess said as she popped open her drink. "I guess I worry too much about things."

"Just let it ride," Casey suggested. He lifted his can in a mock toast.

Smiling, she clinked her can to his.

"Is that a new hat?" he asked after they'd sipped.

She bit her lip as the smile formed. "Yeah," she said, bowing her head slightly, not trying to seem bashful, but impressed that he'd noticed.

"It looks great."

"Thanks. It's what we were picking out when we saw Bran."

"So that trip wasn't a total waste of time."

She felt another smile forming. She hoped it wasn't a silly smile. She bit her lower lip again as she turned to look at him.

Their gazes met, almost too perfectly. She couldn't keep from rolling her eyes and blushing, but after a second, she looked back at him, trying not to giggle.

"You want to take a walk?" he asked. "They'll be busy with the game for a while."

S.W. would probably kill her if she left her for very long in a video game competition with Nathan, but she found herself nodding without hesitation.

"We can make the block," Casey suggested. "It won't take that long. S.W. won't suffer too much torture."

"She'll manage," Tess agreed.

Slipping off the stool, she followed. Casey to the door. The wind was brisk as they stepped onto the stoop, so Tess folded her arms in front of her. Winter hadn't set in yet, but it was on its way.

"You looking forward to Christmas break?" Casey asked as they moved across the lawn to the street where the dusk-to-date lamps were beginning to blaze on.

"It'll be a chance to get a little rest," Tess said. "This business of college prep classes is weighing me down. I can't believe I need to know all this stuff."

"I know what you mean," Casey agreed. "Sometimes I wonder if I want to go to college. I don't know what I really want to do with my life. Sometimes I think I just want to head off across country after graduation, go sightseeing."

"You think you will?"

"I don't own a motorcycle, and I don't think The Judge is up to that long a trip."

"Sounds like it would be fun, though."

"Want to go with me?"

"My folks would never let me."

"You'll be eighteen."

"That wouldn't keep them from killing me. I've already sent out my college applications."

"You going Ivy League?"

"Probably state."

He slipped his hands into the hip pockets of his slacks. "Me, too. Probably."

"Least we'll know each other."

"Yeah."

The street began its curve, and they followed the sidewalk, slowing their pace as if they'd reached an unspoken mutual agreement not to rush the walk.

"Maybe there'll be some good movies this Christmas," Casey said.

"Let's hope. It's been a slow year. I haven't seen many shows in a while."

"Me, either."

They continued to walk in silence, a bit awkward now.

As they rounded the next curve, they moved slightly closer to each other, their shoulders not quite touching.

Casually, Tess unfolded her arms, letting them dangle at her sides. In a way she felt silly, playing little games like this. Both of them had dated before. This shouldn't be that hard, but there just seemed to be steps you had to go through.

His hand found hers only after they had moved the length of the block and were rounding the next corner. She just managed to suppress her grin.

"So you want to do something on the weekend?" Casey asked as they started the last leg of the trip back to his house.

"Sure." Her heart was fluttering, and she didn't want to try more than a syllable.

Still holding hands, they moved across the lawn again, stopping as they reached the stoop at the kitchen door.

"Maybe we can get pizza or something," he suggested. Tess leaned back against the wall beside the door, looking at him in the light of the porch.

He really was cute in his defiant sort of way. He wasn't a real rebel, but he made a good stab at it.

"That sounds good," she said.

He took a step toward her, and she felt her calves trembling. The chill wind had flushed her cheeks and raised goose flesh, but she wasn't in any hurry to go inside.

"After that we could…"

He ran out of words, and they just stood there, looking at each other. The hesitancy made Tess tingle.

Were they going to kiss? Should she let him? This wasn't even a date. Even though she'd wanted him to get interested, this was almost sudden. Did that matter? They were beyond such silly matters.

Some girls at Pembrook wouldn't even bat an eye at the question of kissing at this point, or more.

He moved slowly, leaning toward her. She closed her eyes, waiting. It took forever for the warmth of his lips to come to hers, but when their mouths touched, the thrill of the moment almost made her dizzy. She'd forgotten how long it had been since she'd been kissed.

She kissed back, not wanting to breathe again, not wanting to give up the feeling, the excitement. It was the way romance was supposed to be—spontaneous, unexpected, perfect.

As he moved closer, she slipped her arms around him, pulling herself against him, and the kiss continued. She could feel the warmth of his skin, and the softness of his lips.

She might never have let the embrace part at all if the screams hadn't sounded.

Ten

A Visitor

Bran set his boots on a chair beside the small space heater in the corner of his room, hoping that the warm air would dry them enough by morning.

What a day he'd had.

Laughter from the people in the mall as he'd dragged himself from the fountain pool still echoed inside his head. He'd wanted to break some heads to let them know he didn't like being laughed at, but he'd been so stunned and confused he'd wanted to leave even more.

He'd ridden the bus over to the mall after the incident with Nathan because he hadn't felt like going home once the feeling had returned to his leg. He was too worried to sit in his cruddy little room worrying about what was wrong with him.

Bumming around the mall had seemed like a good idea. If something was really wrong with him, he needed to make the most of his time.

At the mall, there were always girls to watch, and he was pretty good at lifting things he wanted from the shops. Somewhere he had one of those old razor blade necklaces he'd filched just for the heck of it.

He wouldn't be able to snatch a new pair of combat boots very easily, however. He hoped these weren't ruined, but he could already see the leather swelling. He hated that. The old man wasn't going to give him money for new ones, either, and they didn't come cheap.

He didn't have any good way to pick up quick cash, either. Dropping onto the foot of his mattress, he slammed his fist down at his side. What had come over him?

One minute he'd just been standing there, watching the water flow, and the next he'd been climbing over the railing, stepping into the pool.

He'd heard the exclamations and the laughter, but he hadn't been able to stop himself. He'd just moved right in, sloshing around like some goofy kid.

Just before he'd managed to get control of himself again, he'd looked over to see Tess Ryan staring at him, her mouth hanging open in astonishment.

For some reason, he had some odd feeling she was responsible. He couldn't imagine how some little snob who kept her nose turned up all the time could've caused him to jump into a fountain, but he couldn't shake the idea, either.

Maybe he was just looking for someone to blame.

Sliding off the bed, he walked over to the narrow, cracked mirror that hung on his wall. A thin coat of dust had grayed the glass, but he could still see his face clearly.

He looked into his eyes, trying to stare deeply into them to find a hint of what was happening. He didn't know what madness would look like, but he couldn't detect anything out of the ordinary in his pupils. There was no discoloration nor dilation, and his eyes weren't bloodshot.

If someone, like Tess and her friend S.W, had drugged him or something, the drugs had left no residual effects. He turned his back to the mirror and started back to the bed.

He didn't make it before he heard his old man's voice.

"Bran!"

The old man had been out for a drink when Bran had arrived home, but obviously he'd come in now and had probably had time for a conference with the old lady.

Bracing himself, Bran changed direction and moved toward the bedroom door, pulling it open just as his stepfather appeared in the doorway.

"What's going on with you?" he asked. The smell of liquor hung around him, the way it always did.

He was a heavy man with greasy black hair, and his face was covered with a blue-black mask of stubble. Dressed in his dark blue work clothes, he looked weathered yet formidable.

"Nothing," Bran said. He made an effort not to sound meek. More and more he'd been trying to assert himself with his step-father. He wanted the old man to realize he was getting really tired of being pushed around.

"Your mom said you came home soaking wet."

He looked down at Bran's jeans which were still damp from ankles to knees, and then he glanced over to the chair.

"You know how much those boots cost? What'd you do? Just decide to go wading?"

"It was an accident. I..."

Before he could finish, the old man's hand swung in a quick arc, connecting with Bran's cheek and jerking his head to one side. The sting was sharp, but he didn't allow his expression to show it. There might be a red mark, but the old man wasn't going to get the satisfaction of seeing him bat an eye.

"You be careful, whatever you did," the old man said.

Straightening his head, Bran kept his face passive.

That seemed to hack the old man off even more, which was what he'd hoped. He offered only a hard stare as he watched his stepfather's cheeks redden.

"You better straighten up, you understand me?"

Bran squared his shoulders and thrust his chest forward, assuming a stance of attention, then he lifted his right arm and placed his hand against his forehead in a salute.

The old man backhanded him then, the force of the blow connecting so solidly with his jaw that he was almost knocked off his feet. His head was snapped hard to one side, and he stumbled backward, just managing to keep his footing.

"Don't try to get smart with me, boy."

Bran lifted his hand to his face, touching the spot where he'd been hit. He couldn't decide if it was going to bruise or not. Probably it would.

Straightening slowly, he planted his feet, refusing to retreat. He set his stoic expression again and glared at the old man.

"Don't let me catch you doin' anything stupid again," the old man warned. "And don't get smart with me or your mother."

He ambled back out the door before Bran had a chance to respond.

Gritting his teeth and clenching his fists, Bran waited until his anger had subsided before he took a step. He knew if he allowed himself he might run after the old man and challenge him.

Instead, he only walked across the room and closed the door before checking his face in the mirror. His cheek was discolored, but if a bruise formed, it probably wouldn't be a severe one. The blow hadn't been that hard.

If it had bruised, maybe it wouldn't have mattered that much. Whenever he went to school with bruises, people just figured he'd been fighting.

That was part of what had begun to make kids afraid of him a long time ago.

Nobody ever guessed the real source of his bruises, and he didn't tell.

Pulling back from Tess, Casey looked toward the house, but there was no second scream.

"What do you think that was?" Tess asked.

"We'd better check."

Cautiously, he moved toward the door, reaching for the knob. Tess stayed close behind him, watching over his shoulder as he pushed the door inward.

Together, they moved into the kitchen and looked around, but they saw nothing out of the ordinary. All of the cutlery was in place, and no bloody footprints or severed limbs were in view

"Let's check the game room."

Stepping across the kitchen as quietly as possible, Casey shoved the swinging door open.

"Oh no!"

"What is it?" Tess asked as she rushed forward.

Her shoulders slumped with relief when she saw that Nathan was standing on the sofa brandishing a pillow while S.W. attempted to belt him with another cushion.

"What's going on?" Tess asked.

S.W. turned and looked at them. "Nothing."

"She's trying to *moider* me," Nathan said, wiping a hand across his face to feign astonishment. He was joking, but a hint of worry tinged his voice.

Casey walked forward, placing himself between them. "What happened?"

"He sabotaged my game," S.W. protested.

"I did not."

"He jostled my arm because I was scoring more points than he was."

"It was an accident!" Nathan protested, stepping down from the sofa.

"It was not an accident!" S.W. stated. "You just didn't want to get beaten by a girl."

"Did not."

"Maybe we should be going," Tess suggested.

"Good idea," S.W. said.

Casey walked them to the front door, and as S.W. headed for the car, Tess lingered on the doorstep.

"Sorry the kids got out of hand," she said.

"No problem."

"I guess I'll see you tomorrow."

"Definitely."

She felt almost as if she were floating as she moved toward the car.

Nothing was wrong in the world now, nothing she could come up with at the moment.

She wasn't thinking about witchcraft or black magic, and she certainly didn't notice the black cat crouched behind a tree on the front lawn.

Charisse sat in an old padded chair in her living room, looking across the room at the blank wall. If anyone had been on hand to look at her, he might have mistaken her for a wax figure because she was unblinking and unmoving.

Her eyes seemed to strain in their sockets, and there seemed to be a dark glow somewhere behind her pupils.

She felt stronger. Everything was not going as she wanted just yet, but she felt better about herself and about the others.

54

She would've liked to have been included on the shopping excursion she knew S.W. and Tess had taken, but that didn't matter. She had sat thinking, concentrating, and contemplating since getting home from school.

There would be ways to win friends. There would be ways to draw people close to her. She had to be patient, bide her time.

This was a small town, after all. Everything moved a little slower than in the cities where she'd lived, cities such as New Orleans where strangeness was a commodity.

For many years no one had considered her odd there as she had spent her time in the French Quarter and watched the people drift in from the port, people from exotic locales, and people who played games with tarot cards and hoodoo spells.

She tried to remember how she had functioned in small towns before, but that had been a long time ago, a long time and many fallen tears in the past.

Eleven

In Dreams

"So how'd things go?" S.W. asked once they piled into the Buick.

"Fine. Sorry you had to clash with Nathan."

"That was no problem. Details. I want details," S.W. said, twisting sideways in her seat.

"They're not much to tell," Tess said as she backed the car out of the driveway.

"Come on," S.W. protested.

"We walked the block. That's all."

"You went for a walk! That's fabulous."

"It was nothing."

"Nothing didn't smear your lipstick?"

"Is it?" Tess asked, reaching to her mouth as she guided the car through a turn onto Tate Street.

S.W. burst into laughter. "No, but you just confirmed what nothing means. And not even on a date. Whoo."

"We're probably going on a date."

"Well. Then it was a productive evening."

"I don't know."

"Come on. So what if we didn't come up with any answers about Bran and Charisse? You hit it off with Casey. Look at the positive side of things. Forget about all that other stuff."

"I know. I know. I'm not going to think about it anymore. I'm not going to worry about Bran."

"Good, because you've got other things to think about. You're starting a relationship at Christmas time, so you've got to think about presents. You'll want to get him something, but nothing too elaborate."

"I think you're getting ahead of things. Anyway, what if he gets me something really nice?"

"So fine, you're giving, him a token without letting him think you're gaga. Keeps him from getting overconfident. Now, don't forget about Christmas parties. Nancy Gibson is having her usual shindig, and that's what you should go to. There'll be caroling and eggnog. It's old-fashioned, but it's the perfect thing for a party date. You can even slip out early for—"

"That's enough," Tess said. "Let me figure out if he really likes me before you get everything planned out."

"Quit trying to be so cautious. I know you had your heart broken when you dated Dave, but that was eons ago. You've gone too long without dating."

"I said enough," Tess said.

She rounded the corner in front of S.W's house and eased the car to a stop against the curb.

"Just consider your options," S.W. said. She popped the door latch and crawled out. "He's cute. He's cerebral. He's perfect for you."

"We'll see what happens."

S.W. started to slam the door, but before she did, she looked down. "Who's this?"

Bending, she lifted something from the sidewalk. Tess realized that it was a cat, a black cat with green eyes which glowed in the light from the car's ceiling lamp.

"A kitty," S.W. said. "Isn't she cute?"

"It's a black cat," Tess said. "Aren't they bad luck?"

"My grandmother said it was good luck if a black cat came to your house. It's bad luck only if they cross your path."

"Aren't black cats also witch's familiars?"

"Talk about superstition. Quit looking for bad omens."

"Right. Right."

S.W. kicked the door closed and turned back toward her house, cuddling the cat in her arms as she walked. She evidently planned to keep it. Tess felt a little nervous about that.

It was just a cat. But why was it showing up now?

Bran lay in bed, trying to doze but managing instead only to toss and turn. He kept thinking about his old man, and he kept worrying about these odd flashes.

He remembered reading somewhere about fugues, strange moments when the brain lapsed. But a person wasn't supposed to remember what he did in a fugue. Bran recalled everything that had happened to him, every moment.

Rolling over, he closed his eyes, forcing himself to remain still and trying to keep his mind off of illness and insanity. He needed to rest or he would be ill.

Slowly, his mind began to settle, and sleep's foggy mist began to swirl through his head. He was relieved as he realized he was about to doze, and that was his last conscious thought before he found himself dreaming.

He was in the hall at school, and he was in a hurry. He was trying to get somewhere, but he couldn't find the right door.

He kept opening doors and checking inside only to find empty classrooms, or rooms full of nothing at all. He wasn't sure what he was looking for, but he kept searching, moving on and on along the hall that stretched much farther than any of the ones he knew at school. This one was endless, with a supply of doors that never ran out.

He just kept opening them, then slamming them again when he failed to find anything beyond—one after the other until he yanked open the one where the girl stood.

He stopped then, startled. He knew the girl. She was from school, a pretty girl, one of the many pretty girls who'd ignored him. He'd been angry at her for a while, but that had soon faded, becoming only another part of the resentment that simmered inside him—that resentment he felt toward everyone.

He started to close this door, too, but he stopped when she stared at him. Her stare seemed to affect him, making it impossible for him to move as he wanted to.

"What do you want?" he asked.

She laughed. "What do you want?"

"I don't know."

"You aren't very happy are you, Bran?"

"No."

"Why is that?"

"The world's a lousy place."

"You've never had a chance to be happy?"

"Nah, never. My old man's mean. My old lady's a lush, and everybody thinks I'm scum."

"Everyone's had a good laugh at you the last few days."

"Yeah. Usually they're scared of me."

"Too bad you've started losing control."

"I can't figure out what's wrong with me."

"Maybe it's something strange, something they did to you." He looked at her, studying her as she seemed to float in the doorway. White mist coiled around her, and a breeze also seemed to flutter from behind her, toying with her dress and hair.

"How could they?"

"Maybe it's something to think about."

She began to laugh.

Before he could ask her anything else, the door slammed, and he was left standing again in the empty hallway.

A moment later he was back in his bed, sitting up and wondering if what had just happened had really been a dream.

Maybe there was some truth to it. He'd have to check it out. If some of the numbskulls at school had done something to him, he'd get to the bottom of it.

Then he'd get even.

Twelve

Ancient Rituals

Tess met Casey at lunch the next day after apologizing to S.W. and enduring a couple of taunts. S.W. was thrilled that something seemed to be developing between Tess and Casey, but she wasn't going to let Tess get away without some teasing. It was practically required.

After working their way through the line, Tess and Casey selected a table near one of the windows and sat down facing each other. Tess had worn a short, black skirt and dark tights along with a red sweater today, and S.W. had warned her she looked hot. She hoped Casey thought so.

He was wearing a black shirt along with his long black coat, looking more roguish than ever, yet he was wearing his wire-rimmed glasses as well, and that gave him a studious, introspective look.

"How are classes going today?" he asked, as he stuck a straw into his milk carton.

"Not bad."

"Thought about what you want to do this weekend?"

She hadn't been prepared for him to cut to the chase. "I guess we could just get a pizza," she said. "If that's cool with you."

"Pizza's fine. It'll give us a chance to just talk, too."

She wondered if talking was all he had in mind, then almost blushed at her own thought. Fortunately he looked away at about that instant, so he didn't notice.

It was always awkward seeing somebody after a kiss, she thought. She never knew quite how to act. She wondered how Casey felt.

Was she just another cute girl, or did he find her interesting? She didn't know of anyone else that he'd been out with in a while.

Was he looking for something serious? She wasn't sure if that was what she needed since college would be coming up. Something serious might lead to heartbreak, but maybe it was worth taking a chance. She took a bite of the salad she'd been served in order to keep her head from swimming with all of her concerns.

"Looks like Bran's dried out," Casey said, nodding toward the large windows at one end of the cafeteria.

He was standing there with his hands in the pockets of his fatigue jacket. His deep scowl was in place as he stared across the room.

He seemed to be looking for someone, but it was impossible to know what was going through Bran's head. Tess focused her attention on her plate to avoid eye contact. No need to agitate him.

After a second, Casey did the same.

"You looking forward to Christmas?"

"It's not far off," Tess said.

"Yeah, Thanksgiving break wasn't enough time off. Two weeks won't be enough time, either, but it'll help."

"Are you staying in town?" asked Tess.

"Yeah, we've got relatives coming here. My sister will be back from college, and some other folks will visit. What about you?"

"I'll be here."

"I wonder if there will be any good New Year's parties," Casey said. "Last year was a dud."

"What'd you do?"

"I went riding around with a couple of friends. Didn't amount to much?"

"I hung out with S.W. Someone should plan a good bash to ring in the new year."

"Absolutely."

Tess jabbed her fork at some more lettuce. She was hoping Casey was intending to spend some of the holidays with her. Did that mean she was looking for a commitment?

Not at all, she decided. They could just have fun together. The holidays shouldn't be a lonely time. This could shape up to be a pretty good season if things worked out.

She was still playing with her salad when she noticed Charisse drift by. The red-haired girl had apparently finished eating and was headed for the tray return.

She must have eaten alone. She still didn't seem to have many friends. Tess watched her glide gracefully toward the door. She was wearing a black dress that hugged her shapely form, and her hair shimmered as she moved.

Tess felt glad Casey hadn't noticed her. With her ethereal style, Charisse apparently scared some guys off, but she might be the type Casey would find to be a kindred spirit if he took the time to think about it.

Tess wanted to kick herself. Was she getting jealous now? There was no need for that, except that Charisse was really beautiful if you took the time to look at her.

Yes, if Casey took notice of her, she would be jealous. Checking his eyes, Tess decided he still hadn't seen their offbeat friend.

Before she continued eating, she caught sight of Bran again.

He noticed Charisse. Maybe she was the one he'd been waiting for.

He turned and moved after her as she exited the cafeteria.

Tess swallowed nervously. That seemed odd. He could be pursuing Charisse because he hadn't hit on her in a while, but in light of all the other things which had been happening, she felt uncomfortable.

She thought about mentioning what she'd seen to Casey, but she decided against it. She'd dwelled on the ceremony too much. Casey was going to think she was silly if she kept raising apprehensions.

There was nothing to worry about, she told herself. Nothing at all.

It was time to think about her own life. She had enough on her plate, so to speak, to keep her busy.

Bran caught up to Charisse in the back hall. She was busy at her locker, swapping her books from her morning classes for those she'd need in the afternoon.

He approached as she was slamming the door. She tried to ignore him, but he blocked her path.

"What's your hurry?" he asked.

"Lunch is almost over. It's time for my next class."

"I'll walk with you."

She quickened her pace, trying to move away, but he kept moving with her.

"I had a dream about you last night," he said.

"Bran, if this is a come on, it's not working. You're a little too aggressive."

"I dreamed you talked to me?"

"Well dream on."

"I dreamed you told me stuff."

"Did I?"

"That some people were responsible for my feeling weird lately."

"What did I say you should do about it?"

"Nothing. You didn't give me that kind of answer."

"Maybe it's something to think about."

She rounded a corner and started up the hallway. Bran stopped. It was almost like being in the dream again, looking forward at a long line of doors.

He thought about going after her, but he didn't budge. He wasn't scared of her, but he felt uncomfortable again, not as if he were about to do something stupid, just odd.

Something strange was going on. He was going to have to get a grip or he was going to lose his mind.

S.W. and Tess met that afternoon in the library for a study period. Tess was already thumbing through encyclopedias and reference books.

"How was lunch?" S.W. asked.

Tess didn't look up from her books. "Fine, just fine."

"So?"

"Pizza. Definite."

"All right!"

Tess held up a hand to quiet her friend. "Not so loud. We're in the library."

"But it's good news. Tess Ryan reenters the world of the living, and the dating."

"Just keep your voice down," Tess insisted.

"Sorry, I'm just excited for you. Almost as excited as I'd be if I got a date with a neat guy."

"You'll meet someone."

S.W. ran a hand through her hair. "Yeah, with this hair and my weight."

Tess looked at her sympathetically. Sometimes she forgot how self-conscious S.W. could be. "You know how cute you are, and your hair is great. Guys love wild hair. Sometimes I get jealous of you. You can drop a couple of pounds, and you'll be gorgeous. You're already pretty hot."

"Right!"

S.W. flipped open her chemistry book and began to puzzle over a set of equations.

"Don't feel bad about yourself," Tess urged.

"I don't. I'm fine."

"You're sure?"

"Really, I'm fine. I shouldn't have said anything."

After S.W. gave her a reassuring smile, Tess slipped out of her chair. "Well, I'd better get some research done." she said.

Picking up her small spiral notebook, she walked over to the card catalog and began looking up some books for an English class assignment on Percy Shelley.

After she'd written down titles and call numbers, she started for the stacks to track down the books when she had an impulse. She keyed in witchcraft.

Just reading the word made her feel silly. She didn't have any reason to search out any books on occultism. She needed to be busy with her English paper, but she flipped to a different page in her notebook and wrote down a couple of titles.

There were only a few listed, probably because such matters ran the risk of drawing parental protests and being pulled from the shelves. The ones that remained were no doubt harmless, generic books, but after replacing the drawer, she moved over to the 300 shelf.

All of the books on the supernatural were shelved in the 390's, located appropriately in a dark corner at the end of the row of metal shelves. Sliding her finger along the spines of volumes on vampires and werewolves, she finally located a couple of books on magical practices and the occult.

Casey would probably think she was being ridiculous, but a little research couldn't hurt. If nothing else, she might be able to find the book Charisse had used to learn her little ritual. Maybe that would make it clear Charisse wasn't a real witch of any kind.

Tess realized she and S.W. hadn't said much to Charisse since the afternoon ritual. Perhaps they were acting like snobs, their fears preventing them from displaying proper manners.

Slipping a book on the history of magic and the occult off the shelf, she began to flip through it. As she scanned the pages about how cruel men had been to women they suspected of witchery. Tess almost wanted to weep at the cruelty heaped on the innocent because of superstition. She didn't want to duplicate that. She didn't want to be wrong. She flipped through, looking for indication of evil.

The pages were covered with extremely fine print, and she squinted in the shadowy corner, trying to pick up a little meaning from the words. That seemed almost futile. The book dropped in frequent Latin and Greek phrases and discussed ancient rites in Greece and Germany. It all seemed too ancient and cryptic to be pertinent. Then she noticed some odd lettering. Studying it quickly, she realized it was similar to the symbols Bran had scribbled on the chalkboard.

According to the book, a few symbols were Greek or older, and she found other ancient markings which looked forbidding. Bran wouldn't have come up with such characters on his own.

Flipping on through the book, Tess found a list of steps to adopting black arts with an eye toward malevolent sorcery, the kind that gave witches a bad name.

She'd heard of white witchcraft and Wicca, but this seemed to be the other kind, because the list included the renouncing of goodness and light. She also read that a black magic practitioner was required to cut off a piece of a favorite garment in order to show her allegiance to the darkness.

Closing the book, she returned it to the shelf. Some of the business was more about witchcraft of the Middle Ages and superstition, probably more about what they thought they knew about witches in the Middle Ages.

She looked along the row at the other works. None seemed to be very up-to-date. All were the old, library-style books with tape on the spine and faded covers. They'd been here as long as the school had been around, she speculated.

She thumbed through a couple of others, then decided she had nothing pertinent to learn. She turned and was about to head back down the row, but she stopped abruptly.

Charisse was standing there holding books under her arm, but she was looking at Tess.

Walking forward, Tess smiled awkwardly.

"How are you doing?"

For a moment, Charisse continued to stare, her eyes cold and fixed on Tess as if she were trying to look inside her. She blinked an instant later.

"Fine," she said, realizing Tess had spoken. "What are you up to?"

"Just doing some research."

"Me, too," Charisse said.

Tess wondered if Charisse was heading back to check on the magic books. That would make sense. That would mean she'd just read about witches and wasn't really one herself. Maybe she'd even given Bran the symbols as part of the game.

Maybe the rite they'd performed was just some medieval ceremony, more superstition than black magic. That would mean Bran's behavior was normal and there was nothing to worry about. He might even be playing along.

And pigs might be spotted hang gliding around the flagpole.

"Well, I guess I'd better get to work," Tess said, easing past Charisse.

"Me, too," Charisse agreed. She started to turn as well, but before either of the girls could take a step, a loud sound echoed from the end of the bookshelf.

Tess jerked around to look back to the dark little corner. The books she'd been looking at were tumbling off the shelf to the floor, one by one.

Thirteen

Concerns

Charisse settled onto a bench in the commons behind the building. During the lunch hour, the wooden tables were always filled with kids. As they chattered, the sounds of voices echoed off the surrounding building walls and reached an almost deafening roar.

Now it was quiet except for the scrape of a few discarded food wrappers, which slid across the concrete at the wind's whim. For the moment, she liked the solitude. She needed to concentrate without distraction. She looked up toward the sky and watched the winter clouds, heavy and ominous.

Resting her books on her lap, she forced herself to look down at her hands. They were trembling. She had not allowed Tess to see the concern in her eyes, but she could not maintain the facade with herself.

Tess was becoming one of the dangerous ones, one of those who threatened. From the beginning, Charisse had realized that revealing herself could be dangerous, but she had hoped the suggestion and the allure of power would be effective.

She had hoped that the spellcasting would serve a dual purpose, to create a useful pawn in Bran but also to demonstrate to the others what power was all about. She had anticipated winning people over and that they would want to know more.

Instead it had created suspicion. They hadn't been quite as dazzled as she'd expected even though they were young and confused and looking for direction.

She had viewed Tess especially as someone who might be a valuable ally. Unfortunately the girl was proving to be stronger even than Charisse had originally perceived.

She sensed a strength in Tess, a dangerous internal will. She was a person governed by more than desire. If she could not be won over, she would be a formidable enemy, and Tess was looking more and more like someone who could not be won over.

Closing her eyes, Charisse recalled terrors of the past. Sometimes they came in dreams and on other occasions they arrived without warning in her waking—images of skulls and fire and pain.

She had spent many years in hiding, drifting to forget what had come before. The time to regain and regroup had to be selected carefully, but the hour was ticking nearer and nearer.

To turn back would be to forsake all of the forbidden arts she and her sisters had sought to harness. They had given up all for their desires— home, family, society. None of those things had seemed too great, not even when they'd had to flee those who objected to their practices.

If she gave up now, all of it would be in vain. She couldn't forget. She had sworn an allegiance that would not let her forget anymore than it would let her escape.

That's why she had come back in the early autumn, back to the place from which she and the others had departed so long ago to escape the prying of those like Tess Ryan, those who questioned their dark purposes.

She wouldn't let Tess ruin everything now. She could work in other directions. Others were weaker.

As for Tess, if she couldn't be converted, she could be dealt with in other ways.

Fourteen

An Unwelcome Visitor

The Ultimate Pizza at Roland's Pizza Parlor was appropriately named; it had more toppings than anyone could count—peppers, pepperoni, cheeses, sausages, mushrooms, olives, and many other ingredients that didn't make the menu. It was served in a deep pan because it was almost an inch and a half thick.

Tess and Casey ordered a twelve-inch because they didn't feel like tackling a fourteen without starving for a couple of days in preparation.

When it arrived, they pulled slices apart, trying to reel in the strings of cheese that stretched from the pizza back to the pan.

Christmas songs were playing on the juke box, and the place was packed because it was a Friday. Fortunately, they'd been able to find a corner booth that afforded a little privacy. The booths at Roland's had high, ornate wooden backs.

"It's a challenge," Casey said as he wedged some pizza into his mouth. He was looking great tonight in a burgundy sweater, jeans, and his heavy black coat.

"Got it," Tess said, and bit down on her slice. She had dressed in jeans as well with a green turtleneck and her newest black boots. Her jacket was a black blazer which was about a year old, but it still looked stylish and wasn't showing signs of wear.

S.W. had helped her make the selection, noting again how terrific Tess looked while complaining about her own appearance. Tess had tried to reassure her, but it had done no good. She wasn't sure what had brought on S.'W.'s new battle with self-esteem, but it concerned her.

She had too many concerns lately. She wanted to enjoy life. Thinking of Casey gave her a light giddy feeling that came around far too seldom, and she didn't want to waste it.

The pizza was also too good to waste so she forced herself to savor the taste. Tonight, only the things that mattered would occupy her. No Bran, no Charisse, and no S.W.

"You know, Nancy's having her annual Christmas party pretty soon," Casey said as the pizza slices slowly decreased in number.

"Right after we get out for the holidays," she said. "Yeah, which I guess will be week after next."

"Um hum." She was trying to be calm, but she knew what was coming. S.W. had been right, and she had to admit it was a good sign if he was thinking that far ahead.

She felt her stomach tighten as she waited for him to get to his point.

"You want to go?" he asked. "It would be a fun evening. I mean, you kind of catch all the Christmas traditions in one party with Nancy."

"Yeah, it would be fun," Tess said. Nancy hadn't distributed her invitations yet, but they'd be coming soon.

The pizza seemed to evaporate as they continued, talking and eating and gulping soda from huge plastic cups.

For a while, they continued their conversation over the empty tray, but then they decided to vacate.

They had opted to skip a movie, figuring the line would be long on a Friday, the first night of release.

Tess had always felt a movie on a first date was a little bit of a cop out anyway. Sitting in front of a screen for two hours didn't really give much time to get to know another person.

On the other hand a whole evening of conversation could be stressful. Tess was glad Casey was easy to talk to.

As long as she steered away from Charisse and black magic, everything should remain charming. She hadn't mentioned the incident in the library to S.W., and she certainly wasn't going to bring it up to Casey. He'd only dismiss it as happenstance anyway. From time to time, books shifted in libraries and slipped off the shelves.

As they headed for the door, she reminded herself not to dwell on the dark possibilities. She was supposed to be having fun.

Just outside, twin lampposts bordered the door. They had been decorated with brightly colored ribbons. As Tess looked at them, Casey leaned over and kissed her cheek.

She was a bit surprised, and she turned to him. He was smiling, then looked upward.

She was standing under mistletoe. Her astonishment turned to a grin.

"It's tradition," Casey said.

"Right."

He took her hand, and together they walked to The Judge, parked at the corner.

"Where do you want to go?" he asked as they climbed into the front seat.

"I'm flexible."

She didn't slide close to him in the seat, but she felt her heartbeat fluttering. It was their first date. Was she ready to be alone with him?

After starting the engine and pulling out of the parking lot, Casey waved to a group of guys he knew.

It would be easy to suggest he stop to visit, but something kept her quiet. She was waiting to see what he might do. The car kept going.

For a while, they were silent as the car cruised along, its restored engine purring softly as it moved. The radio was functional, yet neither of them reached for the dial.

Tess closed her eyes as the car turned off the strip and moved along a side street which wound through a residential section and back to Arthur Lake.

The road—which curved around trees bordering the lake—was a twisting snake of asphalt, but Casey navigated it with ease. Tess wondered how many times he'd made the trip.

When he pulled slowly off the roadway and guided the car into a cluster of eerie shadows beneath an old oak tree, she realized her insides were trembling.

For a while, as the engine cooled, they looked out through the trees. Beyond the branches the lake was visible, its surface a smooth black sheet with a silver flicker of moonlight.

"It's pretty tonight," Casey said

"Yes." Her voice was only a soft squeak. She'd never felt so demure. She was sitting with her hands folded in her lap. All she needed to do now was bat her eyes, and she'd be the perfect coquette. She felt absurd. She wasn't a freshman. She wasn't immature.

Shifting in her seat, she rested one arm against the seatback. Casey did the same to face her. She hadn't looked so deeply into his eyes in what seemed a long time.

At dinner they'd been concentrating on the pizza. At school there were always distractions, but now it was just them, just the silence.

As he leaned forward slightly, she didn't move. She just let her eyes flutter closed as his lips touched hers.

The kiss was as exciting as the first, maybe more so. As they embraced, she felt the light-headedness again.

None of the boys she'd kissed before had made her feel quite so entranced. She tried to constrain her thoughts merely to keep her head from spinning, yet, she found she wasn't quite in control of her mental or emotional response. Her synapses were firing at will.

As the kiss lingered, she wondered if she were really falling in love. The holidays weren't exactly a rational time. Maybe she was caught up in the festive spirit. Or maybe … or maybe … She was out of excuses.

Casey's hands moved through her hair, letting the long strands slide between his fingers, and she couldn't deny it any longer. Sometimes things just happened.

As she returned the kiss, letting her lips press hard against his, she wondered what she was doing. How could she be falling in love? In one semester she'd be graduating. She'd be going to college. Casey was thinking about the same school, but nothing was definite. If they were in love but didn't wind up in the same school, that might be devastating. How would they deal with it?

And if they did go to the same school, would it be wise to begin college with a commitment? Falling in love now was foolish. She didn't have time to fall in love.

Gently, she eased back, adjusting her position so that she could put her head on his shoulder.

"What are you thinking?" he asked.

"About the whole world," she confessed.

"Not about me?"

"You and the whole world?"

She lifted her head so that she could look at him again as she tried to explain, but she never formed the words. Bran was peering in the driver's window.

Fifteen

Black Magic

When Tess screamed, Casey jerked around to see what she was looking at, but in the second required for him to move, Bran's face disappeared.

Tess wasn't sure where he'd gone.

"What was it?" Casey asked. "I thought you'd seen a werewolf."

"Worse. It was Bran."

"You're kidding."

He looked out into the darkness, but nothing was visible, at least nothing out of the ordinary. Tess checked to make sure her door was locked, then folded her arms around herself.

"It was him."

"Are you sure?"

She wanted to say yes, to be emphatic, but she couldn't be certain. Her thoughts had been spinning. Maybe some subconscious image of Bran had somehow slipped to the forefront of her brain.

"I'm not sure," she said, bowing her head and touching her forehead with one hand. A perfect moment had just been torpedoed, possibly by her own imagination.

Could it be that she'd been so worried about things getting serious that she'd purposely, yet unconsciously, committed sabotage? Did the brain work that way?

She'd read some psych articles, just not enough to really have an answer for herself.

"I'm sure it's okay," Casey said. "You want to leave?" Not really.

74

She didn't want to leave. She wanted to turn back the second hand just a partial turn so the moment could be recaptured.

Since it was lost, she straightened in her seat. "Maybe we'd better go," she said. She didn't want to cry, but she could feel her throat tightening. Why did something have to happen to ruin everything?

She again considered telling Casey about the witchcraft books, but she decided against it. He probably already thought she was loony. She didn't want to give him supporting evidence.

When they reached her house, he walked her to her door, and they stood on the front steps for a moment. "I had a good time," she said.

"Sorry about whatever it was."

"Thanks. I'll talk to you later."

He smiled. "Okay."

The goodnight kiss was just a quick peck, and then he was heading back down the walk. She stepped inside and closed the door, pressing her back against the wall and rolling her eyes.

She didn't have to worry about things getting too serious now. She checked her watch. It was only eleven. That was a sign of a hot date all right. In before curfew. Casey was going to remember her number for sure.

She'd be lucky if he didn't find some excuse not to take her to Nancy's party.

Wiping tears, she headed up the stairs to her room, dropped onto the bed, and grabbed her telephone.

"What's up?" S.W. asked, sounding a little more chipper. Tess quickly went over what had happened.

"You didn't see any sign of him after he looked in the window?"

"No, but he would've gone into hiding. I'm sure I saw him. Well, almost sure I didn't imagine it."

"It was dark, maybe you just saw a shadow or something."

"I think it was Bran, and I think he's getting worse. And more weird. It must have been something we did."

"I thought we were going to quit worrying about Bran."

"I'm trying, but having him play Peeping Tom makes him hard to ignore."

"You're still overreacting to what was just a game. I don't think Charisse is so bad. I talked with her after I left your house, and she seemed pretty nice."

Tess felt her muscles constrict but stifled a gasp. "Where was she?"

"Walking in the neighborhood. I'm not sure who she'd been visiting. She didn't say."

"Did she say anything about the ceremony? Or about Bran?"

"No. We just talked about school and stuff."

Slowly Tess managed to breathe again. "She didn't seem weird?"

"Not at all."

A spooky foreboding descended over Tess. Her fingers tingled as she held on to the phone, and suspicions began to fester in her brain.

S.W. might be trusting, but Tess wasn't sure what to make of Charisse now nor of Bran. The more she reevaluated the afternoon of the candles, the more she believed it could not be just a game devised by Charisse to win friends.

Everything had been executed too precisely. Charisse hadn't fumbled. She'd been sure of herself, and from the way Bran had acted, she had accomplished more than just a spell to make him leave everyone alone. Charisse was playing with him, maybe slowly building up to something with him.

Tess couldn't keep denying that fact. Denying it wouldn't make it go away—even if Casey thought it was stupid and S.W. thought Charisse was nice.

She was going to have to figure out what was happening, and the first step was research. Tomorrow there would be time for that.

After only a couple of more minutes listening to how great Charisse was, Tess rang off with S.W. and changed for bed, selecting an old cotton jersey because of its soft, faded comfort.

After she'd turned out the lights, a mixture of fear and anticipation coursed through her. In the darkness, huddled under the covers, she listened to every creak and moan, wondering if it was the sound of an intruder, but she also contemplated what she might be able to learn.

At least by trying to get a handle on things, she'd be taking action, making an effort to regain control of her life. For the moment, it seemed chaos ruled.

The public library was a majestic old building with huge white columns in front, and a broad row of steps which led up to the entranceway.

After parking the Buick on the street, Tess picked up her notebook from the seat and made her way inside to a very crowded front room.

Students and adults were scattered about the reading tables, and other people wandered in and out of the rows of bookshelves, which stretched back beyond the main room. Still others browsed the magazine and newspaper racks.

Tess hadn't expected so many people on a weekend this close to Christmas. She felt everyone was looking at her as she moved across the carpeted floor, as if they somehow knew she was going to read about something out of the ordinary.

A quick glance convinced her that was only her imagination, and she hurried over to the computer terminal.

After she'd typed in the witchcraft topic heading, a number of titles appeared. She wrote down only a couple that looked interesting, figuring that all of the books would be shelved in proximity to each other as in the school library.

Walking around a cluster of tables and book displays, she proceeded into the stacks. A couple of girls were on the row she wanted to check, but they weren't looking at books. They were busy whispering and giggling. When they noticed her, they moved past and headed for another row.

Nervously, she began to pick through the books. Several of the ones she'd wanted to read were missing, probably checked out. She had to settle for a couple of others, older books with black tape on the spines.

She found herself almost reluctant to pull them from the shelves since she was apprehensive about what she might discover. Only the fact that she was more afraid of not learning forced her to proceed.

She selected a couple of books and headed back to a secluded reading table near the rear of the main room. It was designed to accommodate a single person, so she spread the books in front of her.

From her purse, she slipped out her small notebook. She had recopied the symbols from Bran's chalkboard session inside it. As she began to read, the feeling of apprehension swelled.

Her stomach quivered, and her eyes widened as she took in the words about ancient rituals and practices.

She read of Wicca, the religion in which the members called themselves witches, but that didn't match what she had experienced with Charisse.

Flipping onward, she began to pick up more information, information that seemed to fit with the afternoon ceremony. While the books mentioned white magic, they also warned that since the beginning of time there had been those who had sought dark forces.

She read more, and she could feel the color draining from her face as the words funneled into her brain. She found more markings similar to the things Bran had written. They were commands that a dark sorcerer would send to a victim.

The descriptions of the practices Charisse had utilized were there also—the ringing of the bell, the candles, the markings. All were consistent with the practice of… black magic.

Sixteen

Make-over

Tess didn't connect with S.W. again until Monday morning. Every time she'd tried to call her friend's house over the weekend, she was told S.W. was out.

At school, she finally located her at her locker, and as Tess approached, she was surprised to notice S.W's hair was different. At first Tess thought someone was raiding S.W's things.

She'd had her hair clipped into a short style. All of her unruly curls were gone, and it looked smart and hip.

When she turned around, holding her first hour books, her face was an even bigger surprise. Makeup had been carefully applied to enhance her features without being really noticeable, and as Tess took that all in, she realized S.W. was also wearing a new outfit—a white blouse; a short, red-and-black plaid skirt; and black tights. She looked much more trim. Before she had been cute. Now she was stunning.

"What do you think?" S.W. asked as Tess tried to keep her jaw from dropping.

"You look fabulous," Tess said.

"Think so?" S.W. asked, striking a few poses.

"Absolutely," Tess said. "I guess I can see why you weren't home all weekend."

"Yeah, sorry I didn't call you back. I was a little busy." Slamming her locker, S.W. fell into step with Tess toward their morning class.

"You look like you've lost weight."

"Just the outfit."

"What brought this on?" Tess asked, forgetting the news she'd been desperate to share.

"Charisse thought it would be a good idea."

Tess stopped walking so abruptly that S.W. had moved several paces forward before she noticed they were no longer abreast. She twisted around and came back to the spot where Tess had planted her feet.

"Charisse thought it would be a good idea?" Tess asked.

"Yeah, we got together Saturday, and she started making a few suggestions, so we went to the mall and did some shopping, then we stopped into the salon there and then on Sunday she came over and started helping me with my makeup."

"You're getting chummy with her?"

The frown that rolled across S,W.'s brow was a mixture of puzzlement and anger. "What's wrong with that? We were all going to be friends with her until you got scared by the ritual. She's really a neat person."

"S.W., I tried to call you all weekend because I wanted to explain some things I found out. The stuff we did in that ceremony wasn't white magic. It was black magic. The things Bran wrote on the board were commands. They were probably filtering into his brain when he wrote them. It's real."

"Don't be silly," S.W. said. She started walking again, and Tess had to rush to keep up with her.

"I'm serious. I did some research on the history of sorcery and the rites and practices. Some of the things she did match ancient ceremonies to conjure the forces of evil."

S.W. shook her head. "You're being a little melodramatic, aren't you?"

"No. I'm serious."

"Tess, it's not because I'm being friendly with someone else is it? I'm still your friend, too."

Tess felt her jaw drop again. "How can you think that? I'm glad you did the makeover and everything, but…"

"Are you?" S.W. asked.

"Charisse said you'd probably never suggested a new hairstyle for me or anything like it because you needed a sidekick who could make you feel good about yourself. That's why you always told me how cute my curls were."

A sudden fireball of pain exploded inside Tess as the accusation hit. "You know better than that," she protested.

S.W. shrugged and kept walking.

"I'm sorry if anything I've ever done has made you feel that way," Tess said, hurrying to keep up with her.

"Maybe it hasn't been intentional," S.W. said. "I'm not mad at you. I just thought it might be something for you to consider."

"Wait a minute," Tess said, grasping her friend's arm. "Are you suggesting I'm disturbed?"

"Not necessarily, but you have been getting weird. I mean seeing people peek in your windows while you're making out? If I were with Casey, I don't think that's where my mind would be."

As S.W. disappeared in the crowd, Tess stood almost frozen in the center of the hallway. People flowed around her as she watched S.W's chestnut head bobbing along.

How could she have changed so much since Friday night? She hadn't just changed her appearance. Her entire attitude had been altered.

Tess felt blood rushing through the veins at her temples, and her pulse pounded.

A change that drastic didn't just happen. Closing her eyes to combat the possibility of tears, she slowly composed herself. Only after she'd been able to control her internal quivers did she manage to head for class.

In first hour, sitting next to S.W. was like sitting next to a stranger. She barely acknowledged Tess throughout the period, and she didn't offer to walk with her after that.

Casey was distant also. He was probably still annoyed about Friday night, and he probably wasn't sure how to act toward Tess. They had crossed the line of friendship. Seeing someone the first school day after a date was always difficult, but she hoped everything wasn't ruined.

Tess wasn't sure what she should do. She'd learned only enough from the books to interpret what Charisse had done. She hadn't picked up enough information to be an expert.

She wasn't even sure if she knew enough to convince Casey. She left the classroom feeling bewildered and bruised.

Talking to Nathan seemed to be the best bet. She suspected he'd be a little more open to her ideas about the possibilities of black magic.

She found him just before lunch. He was grabbing some free time in the computer lab where he sat in front of a terminal. The green glow of the letters on the screen reflected across his features, giving him a ghostly look, until he looked up to see her in the doorway.

"What's going on?" he asked brightly.

"Got a minute?"

"Sure."

Tess walked into the room and pulled one of the rolling chairs over to sit beside his terminal.

"I'm worried about Charisse, and everything," she said. With his fingertip, he pushed his glasses back up the bridge of his nose.

"What's happened now?"

"Charisse spent the weekend, practically the whole weekend, with S.W., and she gave her a makeover."

His eyes widened. "Really?"

"I think she brainwashed her, too. S.W. was acting really weird this morning."

"You think Charisse is still up to something?"

"I think so. I think she's had something planned from the beginning. We've got to figure out what it is."

"I haven't seen Bran today. I thought maybe he'd gotten back to just his usual weirdness."

"He's acting worse than that. We've got to do something. We may all be in danger. S.W. in particular, but who knows what she might have planned for us or Casey?"

"Have you talked to Casey?"

She hesitated. She didn't want to go into detail. "Not about this," she said. "Not yet. You know how skeptical he is." She quickly went over what she'd learned from the library.

"Wow," Nathan said when she'd finished. "That really makes it scary. It also explains the strange goings on with Bran."

"Some of them, but he's just part of the problem."

Nathan nodded. "I wish this were a computer problem. I could solve that easy, but this is a little harder to deal with."

"We've got to try to figure out some more about who Charisse is and what she wants." Tess said, leaning toward him and lowering her voice to a whisper because she feared Charisse might happen to walk by in the hallway.

"How do we go about it?" Nathan asked.

"I guess for starters we're going to have to convince Casey. We'll need his help. Then, I think we'll need to do more research, and somehow or other we're going to have to learn something about Charisse's background."

"The holidays will be here soon," Nathan said. "We could use that time."

"We need to get started, but if she doesn't try something before then that will give us some time to try."

She was about to say something more when Nathan suddenly sat bolt upright in his chair.

"What is it?" Tess asked.

Nathan's eyes had widened and frozen into a frightened stare.

Spinning the swivel chair around, she looked toward the door. Bran was standing there, his head slightly bowed and his fierce scowl locked on her.

Seventeen

Missing Pieces

Bran started to move, planning to kick over a chair and then grab for Nathan's throat. He stopped when he saw the fear on their faces.

Tess had an expression of pure horror and Nathan was raising his arms to deflect attack.

He grinned, pleased with that result. Maybe that would let them know he didn't want them playing games with him. They'd forced him to do crazy things before, and he'd heard them conspiring against him here.

He hadn't been able to make out what they were whispering, but he knew they'd been talking about him. Slowly he had begun to understand the message of the dream.

Charisse had come to him again when he'd slept and made it clear, and somehow she had led him here now. She was his friend.

He understood now—Tess and her pals had manipulated him, and he was ready for it to stop. He couldn't think clearly, but he knew one thing. He wasn't going to tolerate any more plotting.

For several seconds, he stood in the classroom, just staring at Tess and Nathan. He wanted them to see he was serious. Neither of them spoke. They just kept watching him, wondering what he was going to do. He let a grim smile continue to play on his lips.

Then words sank slowly into his brain. "What do you want?" It was Tess speaking.

She had stepped forward, still frightened and trembling, but she wasn't cowering.

Bran didn't speak. He just continued his forbidding scowl, then turned and headed for the doorway. He didn't want to talk. He just wanted them to leave him alone.

"Do you know what's happening?" Tess asked.

He didn't answer. He wasn't going to play her games. She knew what was going on. She was the cause of it, her and her wimp friends.

If the craziness in his head didn't end, they were going to pay. They were going to pay dearly.

After watching Bran make his exit, Nathan approached Tess from behind, placing a hand on her shoulder. She shuddered but welcomed his effort to comfort her.

"He thinks we're responsible for what he's doing," she said. "Well, we…"

"No, I could see it in his eyes. He thinks we're manipulating him, making him do things. But it has to be Charisse. She's using him as a weapon to keep us disoriented."

"What does she want?"

"I don't know," Tess said, shaking her head. "But she must have been planning it for a long time. She must have been trying to engineer something even before the ceremony."

"You're just guessing."

"No, think about it. Think back. She dropped little hints about white magic until we consulted her. She wanted us to come to her."

"But what's she doing?"

"I don't know, but it's scary. We're going to have to figure out a way to stop her."

"We'll have to convince Casey it's real, then."

"Yeah. That'll be important. And I've got to try to snap S.W. out of whatever spell Charisse has her under."

"How are you going to do that?"

"I'm going to go see S.W. after school."

As soon as the last school bell rang, Tess made a beeline to S.W's house. She had the Buick that day, and she screeched it around corners until she reached the Wentworth home.

Parking in the drive, she rushed to the door, which was decorated with a new green wreath. She rang the bell, and the door was answered by S.W's mother, a jolly slightly plump version of her daughter.

"Hello, Tess."

"Hi, Mrs. Wentworth. Is S.W. home yet?"

Mrs. Wentworth shook her head. "You want to come in and wait for her?"

"That would be great," Tess said. "We had a little tiff at school, and I kind of wanted to try to make up."

"Oh, certainly," Mrs. Wentworth said.

She ushered Tess into the house and suggested she wait in S.W's room.

Moving into the narrow bedroom, she stood with her hands in her pockets until Mrs. Wentworth disappeared. Then she made a quick sweep of the place. She wasn't sure what she was checking for—voodoo dolls or eye of newt—but she knew she couldn't waste an opportunity.

Stepping softly over to the closet, she carefully slid back the louvered doors and looked inside. S.W's dresses and blouses hung neatly in place, and on the floor her shoes were arranged by pairs. Nothing gross like jars with pickled frogs was in view.

Tess glanced up at the top shelf where some old games were stacked. A couple of other odds and ends were also wedged into place, but she was relieved to see there was no pointy black hat.

Flipping through the dresses, she found most of the items were not new. At least S.W. hadn't gone on a spending spree as part of her makeover.

Quietly closing the closet, Tess stepped back toward the edge of the bed. She wasn't sure what she was looking for. Her attention focused on the chest of drawers, which sat near the window. On top of it along with an assortment of perfume bottles and some loose pieces of costume jewelry sat a night-light which S.W. had owned for as long as Tess could remember. She could see nothing out of place there.

Glancing back at the door, Tess made sure no one was coming, then she stepped softly over to the top drawer. Sliding it quietly open, she looked inside. Some tee shirts and shorts were neatly folded.

The second drawer included sweaters and sweatpants.

In the third drawer she found the scarf. It was silk with a gold and lavender design. Tess had given it to S.W. one Christmas. It had become one of her favorite accessories.

Now a large square hunk of it had been clipped out, leaving a gaping hole. Tess held the fabric in front of her, looking through the opening.

This was no accidental tear. The edges were straight. This had been done deliberately with scissors, and she felt a frigid surge of alarm as she recalled what she'd read in the book on black magic.

As part of the allegiance to the forces of darkness, magic practitioners were required to clip out a portion of a favorite garment. That was the only answer, because S.W. would never have cut the scarf otherwise. Charisse must be working on her, luring her through the steps of becoming a witch.

Tess should never have dismissed Charisse. If she'd been paying attention she could have done something to prevent what was happening. How could it have happened so quickly? Over a weekend!

Charisse had been planning it all along, gradually setting her plan into motion.

Carefully, Tess placed the scarf back in the drawer and closed it into place, trying to cover her tracks. She was going to have to act as if she knew nothing at least long enough to find out what was really going on.

She was starting to step back from the dresser when the loud screech filled her ears. A split-second later she felt the sharp claws digging into her back through the weave of her sweater.

Eighteen

Attacked

Tess jerked her shoulders, arching her back as she yanked her body and arms about in a crazy flutter, trying to shake free of the claws that were ripping at her skin.

Nothing worked.

She felt the soft fur and knew it was the black cat S.W. had discovered the other night. With her eyes closed, she snatched at it, trying to find the scruff of its neck.

She missed on the first couple of tries, and the creature tore at her back, trying to rip her to shreds. The tiny claws were vicious weapons.

Finally, her fingers found the loose fur, and she gave the cat a hard tug, pulling it free even as it continued to hiss and screech. The claws pulled at the threads of her sweater, but Tess didn't care about the damage.

With a flick of her arm, Tess tossed the animal over to the bed where it landed on its feet in the center of the mattress. The bedsprings creaked in protest. The cat was larger than she had realized.

In a matter of seconds it had turned again, and before she could even begin to move for the door, the beast lunged.

She lifted one arm to protect her face, and the claws dug through her sleeve. She felt a searing pain in her forearm and realized the claws were drawing blood.

Frantically, Tess shook her arm, trying to dislodge the frenzied attacker, but the cat clung fiercely, refusing to let go.

Again, Tess had to reach for it, and grasping it again by its dark fur, she tugged. The cat didn't release, but she gripped it even harder and yanked at it until the claws gave way.

When she released the cat in midair, it twisted about and landed on the carpet, this time turning and scampering toward the door.

Tess was left looking at her arm. The knit of her sweater had been ripped, and her arm was sliced open. Blood coursed out of the wound, a narrow fissure which stretched from just beneath her elbow almost to her wrist.

Remembering first aid instructions about applying pressure, Tess pressed her thumb down on the spot where the blood seemed to be spurting, but that didn't seem to do much good.

The blood continued to flow, spraying around her fingers and running down her forearm. She prayed the cat hadn't severed something important, but through the blood, she couldn't really tell how badly she was hurt.

As she tried to step toward the bedroom doorway to call for Mrs. Wentworth for help, dizziness rippled through her head. She was losing it.

Black spots appeared before her eyes, huge black spots that grew larger and larger and began to merge with each other.

She had a sense of losing balance, of tumbling forward, but then everything seemed to shut down, and the blackness became total.

———

When Tess's eyelids finally fluttered open again, she could see only a bright white light. It was a huge, round orb of radiance glowing over her head.

Slowly, she lifted her arm, reaching toward the light, uncertain of where she was or where she was going. Was she adrift in some celestial sea?

Something tugged at her arm as she tried to extend it, something that seemed to be trying to hold her back from the light. She tried even harder to reach upward, and she felt a grip of pain.

Before she could make another attempt, a hand closed around her wrist, gripping tightly and endeavoring to pull her arm down. She tried to pull her arm away, but they gripped tightly.

"Hold still."

The reality of the voice jarred her consciousness.

Blinking to clear her eyes, she tilted her head to the left, toward the sound.

A nurse in a white uniform and cap was standing there, holding her arm and trying to adjust an I.V. Beside the nurse, a plastic saline bag hung from a metal stand. "You're going to pull the needle out," the nurse warned. She was young with short, dark hair, but she was stem.

"Sorry," Tess said groggily. "I didn't…"

She jerked her head up from the pillow and the pain almost exploded inside her skull. Letting her head rest again, she rolled her eyes around in their sockets.

She was in a hospital room.

"You've lost a lot of blood," the nurse said. "We're trying to replace some of it. You need to settle down."

"How'd I get here?"

"I'm told your friend's mother found you and dialed 911. You're lucky."

Tess looked down at her other arm and realized it was bandaged.

"Fifteen stitches," the nurse said.

"From a cat?"

"We weren't sure what got hold of you," the nurse said.

Tess's parents had been waiting in the <u>hall</u> while the nurse performed her duties. They returned when she stepped outside and spent some time talking. Tess tried to remain bright and cheerful.

"There's someone else here to see you," Mrs. Ryan said after a while. "He's been waiting with us for you to wake up."

Her eyebrows arched. "Who?"

Her father went to the door and pushed it open, and Casey stepped in wearing his long black coat and black motorcycle gloves, the kind without fingers. Her dad didn't seem to notice even though he was usually prone to wrinkle his brow and shake his head at what he considered rebellious attire.

With a slight smile, Mrs. Ryan stepped back from the bedside. "We'll let Casey talk to you awhile," she said, "but if you need anything, we'll just be getting some coffee."

"I'm fine, Mom. Just a little drowsy."

"That's probably the medication," Mrs. Ryan said. "Try to stay awake for Casey."

"I'll try."

As her parents exited, Casey moved to the side of the bed and rested his hands on the railing.

"What happened?" he asked.

She sat up slightly, even though the movement made her head spin. "I was attacked by S.W.'s cat."

"I didn't know S.W. had a cat."

"She hasn't had it long. I don't think it's really a cat."

He laughed. "You don't? What do you think it is? The drugs really are getting to you."

"It's not the drugs. I know you're skeptical, and I've tried not to bother you with my worries, but you've got to listen. I think that cat is a familiar."

"A what?"

"A familiar, a conjurer's connection to the dark side. A liaison with…"

"We're back to Charisse again?"

"Yes, we are. Have you seen S.W.? Charisse gave her the makeover."

"I know. She looks great."

Tess felt a twinge of jealousy but quickly submerged that feeling. "How long have I been out?"

"Since yesterday. They said it was just exhaustion and dehydration."

"She wanted me out of the way," Tess said with a sudden realization.

"Who?"

"Charisse. She's making S.W. part of her circle. I found a ruined scarf at S.W.'s. I read in one of the black magic books that a dark practitioner offers a portion of her own clothing to the spirits of evil."

"Right." Casey gave her a skeptical look.

"Casey, it might sound outlandish, but it all fits together. Black cats, a drastic change in S.W., Bran. It's Charisse, and she's up to something. I need your help. I shouldn't have been out this long, should I? She took my blood at the ceremony. She's probably got me hexed."

"You really think there's something to this black magic business? The way it appears, Charisse tried the white magic route with us so we'd think she was interesting. She wanted to get us to be her friends, that didn't work, so she's suddenly a beauty expert, and it's won S.W. over. Next week she'll be something different. You've known that kind of person."

"I know, I know! Sally Rexmer is that kind of person, but that's not what we're up against. Charisse is evil. I can feel it!"

Casey lifted his hands. "Okay, okay. What do you want me to do?"

"Get some more books on black magic, and talk to Nathan. We've got to try and figure out where Charisse really comes from and what she wants."

"Okay, we'll start doing some checking. You just rest."

"I will, but just trust me."

"I'm trusting you." He reached over and took her good hand.

"I'm here for you," he promised, giving her hand a squeeze. "Get well so we can make it to the Christmas party. The invitations are going out this week."

He was about to lean forward to kiss her when the door suddenly swung open, crashing back to the wall with a loud crack.

Then S.W. marched into the room. She was wearing a short denim skirt and a new sweatshirt, and she looked as gorgeous as the last time Tess had seen her, except that her face was red and her eyes were bulging.

She was angry, livid, and she seemed as if she was going to climb up onto the bed and go for Tess's throat with her fingernails.

Nineteen

After Hours

"Do you know what happened?" S.W. asked angrily.

Tess wasn't sure what she meant. She shrank back against her pillow, gripping Casey's hand, glad he was there.

"I don't know what you're talking about? I was waiting—"

"I'm not talking about your breaking into my room," S.W. said. "That was bad enough, but I mean this." She reached into the pocket of her skirt and pulled out a piece of red construction paper which had been cut in the shape of a Santa.

"The invitation," Casey said.

"My invitation," S.W. said. "I got one. You guys got one. Everybody got one but Charisse. Why do you suppose that is?"

"Maybe Nancy just doesn't know her very well yet."

"Or maybe you told her you didn't want Charisse to come because you're still jealous," S.W. said with an accusatory glare.

"Come on, S.W.," Casey protested. "You know Tess wouldn't do that. She's been here in the hospital."

"There's a telephone on the nightstand. She could've called Nancy last night. Or they could have hatched a plot before all of this."

"I didn't do anything to try and stop Charisse from being invited to anything," Tess protested. She was feeling dizzy again, but she forced herself to be assertive.

"You didn't like her," S.W. protested. "That's just as bad." Casey stepped over to S.W. "Come on," he said. "Calm down. Tess has been through a lot."

"Well she deserves it," S.W. said, spinning and heading for the door.

Tess lowered her head to the pillow. She didn't feel well at all. Her stomach was upset, and she felt a tightness in her chest.

Only part of it was due to having her best friend attack. She'd heard people say it was better not to dabble in magic, but she'd never thought their little foray into spell-casting could have caused so much harm.

"You all right?" Casey asked, returning to the bedside. "You look really pale."

"I guess that just upset me." She began to feel cold chills wracking her body.

"Well, it kind of convinced me something strange is going on," Casey agreed. "S.W. really isn't herself."

"Neither am I, and I don't think it's blood poisoning," Tess said in a weak voice.

As her eyelids grew heavier, and the tightness seemed to worsen, she tilted her head in Casey's direction.

"You'll help?"

"Yeah, sure."

She was about to thank him, but she couldn't get the words out of her mouth, probably because at that moment her breathing stopped.

"The doctor said it was septicemia?" Casey asked.

He was sitting in a small chair next to Tess's bed in her room at home.

Tess looked up at him weakly. "Yeah. That's a kind of blood poisoning from the cat scratch. I have to stay in bed another day. Mom's already talked to the principal. Looks like I won't be going back until after the holidays."

"You're lucky you got to come home."

"They were ready to get me out of the room, I guess. I scared them, though. The doctors said they'd never seen an infection crop up that quickly, and they'd already given me some shots."

"Guess it wasn't your average cat," Casey said.

"Guess not. You sound a little less skeptical."

"Maybe I am."

With difficulty, Tess shoved her elbows against the mattress, pushing herself upward. "Why?"

"Your little respiratory arrest scared me. When the doctors rushed in, I just started thinking that the whole thing couldn't be natural. I tried to do some checking like I promised, about magic, but when I went to the school library the books were all gone."

"They were there, I know."

"I asked the librarian if someone had them checked out, but there was no record of that. The books have just disappeared."

"I should have grabbed them the other day."

"Not to worry," Casey said. "I've got someone on the job as we speak."

"Who?"

"Nathan. He's been reading a web forum that specializes in the arcane. He's been posting notes and gathering information for a couple of days."

"What's today?"

"Friday, babe." He quickly belted a chorus of the ancient Alice Cooper tune, "School's Out." Along with his other rebellious traits, Casey had eclectic taste in music.

"Wow. I've been out of it so long. Almost a whole week."

"You've had a bad—"

"No, not a bad case of anything real. I think Charisse had something to do with it. She's poisoning my blood. And I even gave her some like a fool?"

He reached over and brushed a couple of locks of hair from her brow. "Maybe you're right about that. My skeptic's nature tells me this could all be a delusion from your sickness, but something else tells me there's more to it than imagination."

She took his hand and squeezed. "We have to figure out what to do."

"I know. So far we haven't exactly come up with easy answers."

"You can find ways to kill a vampire. Aren't there ways to deal with a sorceress?"

"Not exactly. Most of what Nathan has picked up comes from people who want to point out either that magic practitioners aren't all bad or that witches have always been tortured way in the past."

"Tortured?"

"Well, there were people tortured for supposedly practicing witchcraft. You know about Salem. He's also mentioned something about Louisiana. I'm not sure what happened there."

"Wow."

"Innocent people suffered in Salem. And in Europe, too, during the Inquisition. But Nathan's also gathering some other information. Apparently real evil magic practitioners are harder to spot."

"Because they're more reluctant to show themselves."

"Exactly. Most of the people who have been persecuted with as witches in the past weren't witches or magical practitioners. They were victims of superstition and stupidity."

"So the lore isn't accurate, and we don't have any way to fight Charisse."

"There's a way. We just have to figure out what it is."

"Maybe we should find a priest and get some holy water."

"We'll see what Nathan finds out."

She squeezed his hand. "Thanks for believing."

"Don't mention it. I'm with you. We'll figure it all out."

"I'll be up and around soon. I'll be fine."

"Yeah, and we should be hearing from Nathan. Hopefully he'll come up with something."

Even though school was officially closed, Nathan stayed after hours in the computer lab, hunched over his keyboard.

He was supposed to be out to the building already, but he hadn't want to stop his effort.

Now he was scanning responses to messages he'd left earlier on the board in a couple of categories, hoping to elicit responses. Several replies were jokes from skeptics who didn't put much stock in the supernatural.

He ignored those, scrolling on through the list, scanning for serious answers. A reply from a man in Chicago seemed to take him seriously. The heading read: From FATHER ALISON.

Greetings Nathan, it read.

His eyes moved from side to side quickly as he began to read:

> *Your interest in esoteric matters seems more than a*
> *passing fancy. If you have indeed encountered someone*

from ancient orders you might have a true problem. My
friend Vinoba and I have devoted our lives to researching
such matters. Some of the practices you've mentioned do
resemble ancient rituals, perhaps dating back as far as the
Ovates, a group of witches from France, though it would
appear to be a twisted version of …

A sound broke Nathan's attention. He swiveled his chair around to peer back at the door, but he saw no sign of anyone. Maybe it was time to get out of here. He hit the print command, and a second later the printer across the room began to spew paper. Father Alison had written a lengthy note, so the printer stayed busy for several seconds.

When it was finished, Nathan shut the computer down and made a quick trip over to grab the sheets from the page. He could read it later or share it with Tess and Casey.

Folding it quickly, he tucked it into his pocket, then gathered up his books and headed for the door. While all of the exits would be locked, fire regulations required that they open from the inside.

He could go out any door he needed to. He just had to make it to one of them. He hurried along the hallway toward the front exit, the one closest to the computer room.

As he moved, he tried to listen for approaching footsteps, but only his own seemed to echo along the vacant hallway.

Glancing back over his shoulder, he could see only the darkness and shadows of the rows of lockers. At least no one was following him.

He rushed on toward the beacon of the green and white EXIT sign over the dual doors and hurled his weight at one of the bars, which would activate the latch. The bar gave easily, but the door opened only a fraction of an inch. Then it clanked and refused to budge any further.

Nathan leaned into it again, trying to force it, but he had no luck. That wasn't supposed to happen. With another shove, he attempted to force it, but again it refused to open.

He moved over a few inches and tried the other of the dual doors, but it also wouldn't budge. Examining the lock, he realized someone had wrapped a chain into place so that the doors wouldn't open. An old bicycle lock held the chain in place.

Bran chuckled as he watched the wimp try to pull the lock open. He didn't have a chance. The little punk always thought he was so smart, but he was about to learn. He wasn't smart at all.

Bran's thoughts were a jumble, but he knew what he had to do. He focused on his mission. For several days he had been lost in a daze, but now everything was perfectly in order.

He'd been confused because he hadn't wanted to turn himself over to the impulses in his head, so he'd had several demonstrations.

Now he wasn't fighting. He knew he had orders to follow. He knew he would take revenge on those who had played games with his destiny, and then he would do whatever he was told.

He had a purpose now, for the first time.

The lock wasn't something that one of the janitors would have put in place. Nathan whirled around, realizing something was drastically wrong. He prepared to make a dash for one of the other exits.

He didn't get to take a step because Bran was standing only a couple of inches away in his socks.

"Thought you might try to get out that way," he said. "What's going on?" Nathan asked.

"I know what you're up to," Bran said. "You've been on that computer drumming up magic spells to put on me."

"You've got it wrong. I'm trying to find a way to break spells."

"I know what's going on. You and your pals are out to destroy me."

"Who told you that?"

"I had a vision, a dream. I know what's happened, and I know what's going to happen."

"That's crazy Bran."

"I'm following Charisse's will."

"You're nuts."

"No, I'm not."

"She's some kind of sorcerer."

"A witch's gotta have an assistant."

Nathan tried to run, but he didn't get far. Bran came after him, grabbing a handful of Nathan's hair.

Before he could pull away, Bran's hands closed around his head, pulling upward, yanking.

Nathan's scream snapped off in mid-syllable.

Twenty

An Early Christmas Present

Tess awoke with a fitful twist, and she realized she was tangled in the covers. Though she couldn't remember it, she'd apparently had a bad dream. Sweat covered her, soaking her gown so that it stuck to her skin. A feeling of anxiety lingered over her.

Sitting up, she pulled back damp locks of hair, trying to recall what had filled her thoughts a moment before. She found only the impression that she had witnessed something horrible.

As her heartbeat slowed, she realized how thirsty she had become. Maybe she'd had another round of fever. Regardless, she was going to have to go down to the kitchen for some juice.

She slid her feet into fuzzy pink slippers. They were soft and comfortable, and their familiar texture consoled. Familiar things were always nice in moments where the world seemed to be turned around.

The clock on the bedside read 3:05 A.M. She needed to get something to drink and then try to get back to sleep.

Without turning on a light, she felt her way across the room and eased the door open to step into the hallway. A small night-light glowed in the outlet, making it easy to find the staircase.

Although she still felt a little weak, most of the dizziness was gone, and she was able to climb down the steps without stumbling.

As she moved through the front room, she was surprised to see the Christmas tree was in place, and the lights were flickering reds, golds, and greens, a rainbow of shadows.

She didn't have to turn on the ceiling light at least. She looked at the decorations for a moment, then ducked into the kitchen.

Her mom must have decided to put the tree up while Tess was in the hospital, probably to cheer her up when she returned. The family tradition was to wait until close to Christmas Day to trim the tree.

Someone must have left it on by mistake because it couldn't be a good idea to have an unattended tree on in the middle of the night. Tess decided to unplug it before returning to bed.

After gulping a quick glass of orange juice, she shoved the kitchen door open again and moved back into the living room.

She had to give her mom credit. She'd done a beautiful job on the tree. As the lights bounced off the shiny ornaments, Tess felt a little spirit of the season, the first real feeling of Christmas she'd had this year. For a moment, she stood, watching it, enjoying the flash and the glow of the colors and hues.

A yawn reminded her she needed to be trying to rest, however. She wanted to be alert tomorrow so that she could work with Casey.

It was time to turn off the tree and head back upstairs. She moved toward it slowly, trying to figure out where the plug was. That was the only way she knew to power down the Ryan collection of lights. Finally she knelt beside the tree and began to push branches back, searching for the cord.

Her eyes widened when she touched something solid beneath the tree. Surely no one had put presents there yet.

Finally grasping one of the low branches, she pulled it back.

She found herself looking into Nathan's eyes. They were frozen and glazed, offering back a black stare of nothingness.

For a second Tess tried to figure out how he'd managed to get into such an odd position, and then she realized that only his head was present.

She began to scream. And scream. And scream.

When Tess awoke, she was in her parents' room. Her mother was sitting of the edge of the mattress, and her father stood beside the bed, both looking worried.

Sitting up, Tess tried to babble a warning about what she'd seen, but her mother quickly pressed her back to the pillow.

"Calm down, sweetheart. Everything's all right."

"Did you call the police?" Tess asked.

"No, sweetheart. You just had a bad dream. You may have been walking in your sleep."

"We found you on the living room floor," her father said.

"I saw Nathan's head."

"What?"

"Nathan's head was under the tree!"

"Try to calm down and get ahold of yourself. You saw a trick of the light, and your imagination did the rest."

"Right, sweetheart. There's nothing like that down there," her mother said.

"You've got to check," Tess insisted. "I saw it. I didn't imagine it."

Mrs. Ryan turned back to look at her husband. Silently, they conferred by arched eyebrows. Finally, Mr. Ryan agreed to go and check just to put Tess at ease.

While they waited for him to return, Mrs. Ryan took Tess's hand and patted it gently. "It's okay. You've had a rough time of it."

"It's not just my imagination or my being sick. Something really strange is happening."

"Please settle down, dear. Christmas is coming. You'll have time to rest. You need to get your strength back. Casey told us you're going to a party."

"Mom, that's several days away. Besides—"

"There's nothing there," Mr. Ryan said, stepping back through the bedroom doorway. "I crawled all around the tree, and I didn't find anything but the tree skirt. Besides, there would be blood everywhere if there'd really been a severed head there."

"I put the tree up because I thought you'd like to see it," Mrs. Ryan said. "I thought it would cheer you up. I didn't mean to upset you."

Tess let her head sink into the pillow. She hadn't imagined it, but there was no convincing them. How long had she been unconscious? Long enough for someone to put the head there and then take it away?

She sat up quickly. "You've got to check the house, Dad. Someone may be in here. It may be Bran. He's been acting crazy the last few days."

"Sweetheart, there's no one in the house. You've had fever."

"You've got to check."

After flashing a look of exasperation at Mrs. Ryan, he turned and headed out the door again.

Mrs. Ryan continued to sit on the bedside, softly stroking Tess's hair. "It's going to be fine."

Tess wanted to believe her, but she couldn't relax until her father returned. He was gone a long time, an eternity.

"I checked all the doors, and I looked everywhere," he said when he returned. "There's nothing there. Really."

With a sigh, Tess let her head settle back on her pillow, but she kept her eyes open, staring up at the ceiling.

Her parents might not believe it, but she'd seen the head, and she knew something was very wrong.

She would try to call Nathan tomorrow, but she knew she wouldn't find him at home.

Twenty-One

The Old Dark House

Casey came over after breakfast the next morning. He was wearing a black shirt and a faded denim jacket that today drew Mr. Ryan's scowl, but he ignored the disapproving glance.

Tess was already showered and dressed in jeans and a red and green sweater she'd had since last Christmas.

Her hat would have matched it, but she couldn't bring herself to put it on. It only made her think of S.W., and that was painful. Her best friend was becoming a sorceress, and there didn't seem to be anything she could do about it.

As soon as she could pull him aside from her parents, she told Casey about the nightmarish events.

"I didn't dream it. I know I didn't."

"But you didn't find any blood? No signs of a break-in?"

"No, but that doesn't mean anything. Charisse could've used spells, couldn't she?"

"Maybe she just projected the mental image into your head."

"Have you talked to Nathan yet today?"

"No. I was supposed to check in with him. He was doing some computer work that was supposed to dig up some answers.

You know how he gets when he starts talking about the computer underground and everything."

"A message board's not really the computer underground, but let's check on him."

"Okay. Let me call."

He sat with the cell pressed to his ear and waited a long time before someone answered.

"Nathan's mother," he mouthed silently to Tess just before introducing himself.

"I was wondering if Nathan is around."

A frown crossed his features. "Not since yesterday?"

He listened for a couple of minutes and began to voice reassurances.

His face was pale as he hung up. "She hasn't seen him since he left for school yesterday. She's talked to the police, but they haven't found him yet. They think he may have run away."

Tess knelt beside Casey's chair and gripped his forearm. "That means what I saw could've been real, not just a nightmare."

Casey closed his eyes. "I'm afraid so."

"Is it our fault?" Tess asked.

"No. We all went into it together. Charisse is to blame if anyone is."

"We've got to find a way to stop her."

Casey pulled himself out of his chair and walked to the window, looking out at the overcast day. "I'm open for suggestions."

"We've got to learn more about her," Tess said. "We know she's a witch, but what else do we know? Nothing. We don't know where she came from, what she's after."

"Our hides, apparently," Casey said.

"Maybe, but is that all?"

"What do you want to do?"

"Search her house."

"That could be pretty dangerous."

"We're already in danger. Think about it. Besides, we can be careful. She's hanging out with S.W."

"What about parents?"

"I don't think she has parents. We haven't seen any."

"So you want to go stake the place out?"

"Why not? We could watch and see if any parents show up."

"We could get arrested if we break in there."

"What if we break in and find Nathan's body. Then the cops would thank us."

"Maybe." Casey shrugged. "Why not? Everybody thinks I'm a hood anyway."

They parked the Buick under an oak tree a block away from Charisse's house, figuring it would be less conspicuous than The Judge. The leaves had fallen from the tree, but its branches still cast a few concealing shadows. Tess hoped that at a distance they would help obscure the car.

As they sipped malts they'd picked up on the way, they waited, watching cars pass occasionally. The neighborhood was generally quiet.

For a long time, they saw no sign of life or movement in the house, so they listened to a CD Tess had bought last spring. Listening to the fast-paced lyrics made her remember listening to the disk when it was new.

That had been a long time ago now, and looking back it seemed like a wonderfully uncomplicated time. S.W. had been her buddy, they'd been looking forward to their senior year. Now everything was going wrong.

Things changed quickly.

She was snapped back to reality when Casey reached over and shoved her downward. "Duck," he said.

Without hesitating, she pulled down in the seat, joining him in a contorted position on the floorboard.

"What is it?" she asked, bending uncomfortably around the steering wheel.

"I saw S.W. pulling into the driveway," he said. "I don't think she saw us."

"This could be what we were waiting for."

"I know."

"Maybe we should've done this at night."

"Did you want to go in there at night?"

"Guess not."

"Besides, this is the perfect time. Nobody expects burglars on a Saturday."

After a few seconds, he eased himself upward slightly to peer over the dashboard.

"They're driving away together," he whispered, though there was no danger of unwanted listeners.

"Maybe going shopping."

"Or to bury Nathan's body," Casey suggested.

He watched for several seconds, then looked at Tess with a nod. "They're gone. Let's move."

"Lead on," Tess said, pulling herself from her crouched position and dusting her jeans.

They climbed out of the car slowly and walked side by side, trying to look like just a couple of kids out for a stroll.

Tess felt arctic swells flowing up over her vertebrae as she and Casey strolled up the Bienville driveway. She couldn't help being nervous. She didn't have any experience at breaking rules, but she had no choice. She had to think of S.W. and Nathan and other people who might be hurt.

Together, they climbed onto the front porch and walked to the door, just a couple of Charisse's friends checking to see if she was home.

Casey curled his fingers into a fist and hammered on the front door. Then they waited, hearts fluttering as seconds ticked past.

When no one appeared, he hammered again, louder, trying to make sure that if someone was inside they'd hear the knock. The last thing they needed was to find a way inside only to surprise someone who'd been sleeping or showering.

"Nobody's home," Tess said.

"Apparently not," Casey whispered. "Let's see if we can find an open window."

He tried the front knob, just to make sure it was locked. If they squeezed in a back window and then learned the door was open, they'd feel stupid.

The lock was in place, however, so they left the porch and headed around back. All of the windows there were latched, so they wound up squeezing through one of the narrow basement windows.

Being back in the room where the first ceremony had been performed seemed eerie. Tess looked around the shadowy room as Casey lowered himself down beside her, and for a moment, she relived the ritual in her mind.

If only she could go back and convince herself not to participate. That would have made all the difference.

She knew there was no point in even thinking about that, however. They had to deal with reality.

"Isn't this how kids in horror movies always get bumped off?" Tess whispered as they moved across the basement floor.

"They're just not careful enough," Casey said, reaching for her hand.

They made their way through the shadows as quietly as possible and paused at the base of the stairs. "Do we go up?" Tess asked.

"That's what we came for."

The stairs creaked under their weight as they began to climb. "Easy does it," Casey whispered.

"If nobody's home it shouldn't matter."

"Maybe not, but we don't want to stir up any demon guardians."

He was being sarcastic, but Tess massaged her still bandaged forearm. "Tell me about it."

Moving as silently as possible, they made their way to the first floor, and Casey eased the door open, peering through it cautiously.

"Looks safe," he said, leading the way into the kitchen.

A thin coating of dust seemed to cover everything in the room, and a musty odor of neglect hung in the air.

"It's like nobody's used this room since we passed through the other day," Casey said.

"Really. It's spooky."

They moved into the living room. It was also dusty, though there were a few other signs of life. Charisse's schoolbooks were stacked at the center of the room, and a few other items were strewn about.

"You can tell where she spends her time," Casey said. "She may be living here alone," Tess said. "Fooling us about her family."

"I'd say that was the case," Casey said. "This place isn't occupied by a family. It doesn't feel right."

A search of a few other rooms confirmed those guesses. Rooms were either empty or seemed not to have been disturbed in ages, and there were almost no signs of personal items—no family pictures, trinkets, magazines, or even junk mail.

"This is really odd," Casey said.

He was about to head for the stairs when Tess screamed.

Twenty-Two

Cops

The cat had approached silently, perching on the second-floor banister to watch them move about. The sight of them climbing toward the second floor prompted it to action.

Launching itself off the railing, it sailed toward Casey with claws extended and a wild look in its eyes.

Tess's exclamation reached him just in time. He jerked out of its way, and the needle-like claws missed his eyes by a couple of inches. Instead the cat hit lower, the nails digging into Casey's scarf.

Screeching, the cat tried to untangle itself, but Casey unfurled the fabric from around his neck and tossed it away, letting the angry feline become even more ensnared.

Fitfully it struggled, and when it finally managed to free itself, it darted across the living room and disappeared through the kitchen doorway.

"Guess he was left to guard the second floor," Casey said.

"Just like at S.W.'s. It's the same one. Must be something up there we shouldn't see," Tess said, raising a hand to her heart as if the touch might slow her rapid pulse.

"Let's go check," Casey said. He took her hand again, and they moved upward, pushing open doors on the second floor and finding another array of empty and neglected rooms.

They were about to give up when they shoved open the door at the end of the hall. It seemed to be the room in which Charisse was living.

A bed with a fresh spread sat against the wall, and some of Charisse's discarded clothes were tossed across a chair. More schoolbooks were stacked up here, and near the window there were also shelves.

Lining those were numerous jars filled with cloudy liquids, preservatives for the various roots and leaves stored inside the glass.

"What is all that?" Casey muttered.

"Herbs," Tess whispered. "At least they seem to be herbs."

"Eye of newt and that kind of thing?"

"It's probably the kind of stuff that started the rumors about eye of newt," Tess said. "The reality that birthed the legends."

"Did you read that in one of the books?"

"Something to that effect."

She stepped cautiously over to the shelves and scanned the jars. She wasn't good at plant identification, but she had a feeling this information might be useful.

Selecting a jar containing a particularly gnarled specimen, she held it up to the light which streamed in through a slit in the ragged curtains over the window.

"Recognize it?" Casey asked.

"No, but I think we're narrowing the field."

"How so?"

"If she uses herbs, that might help us figure out what kind of practitioner she is, or what she spun her dark magic off from. We'll have to go back to the library."

"You think we're going to find anything else?"

Carefully, she replaced the jar as she had found it. "We've been in here long enough. Maybe this will give us something to go on.

Hurriedly, they made their way out of the house, and once they were outside, they tried to walk quietly to the Buick although they really wanted to break into a jog.

They drove to the library and luckily found it wasn't crowded, so they gathered the books they wanted and selected a table. "What exactly are we looking for?" Casey asked as he thumbed through a thick text.

Tess shoved aside an old Time-Life book she'd been examining and picked up an older volume with a cracked spine.

"Something about herbal medicine or whatever. She obviously uses that as part of her magic."

Casey flipped to the back of the book, scanned the index, and then tapped the page. "Herbs, use of."

"See what it says."

He turned to the designated page and began to read through the material.

"Herbs were utilized in a variety of rituals including voodoo practices as well as other ceremonial observances. A particularly feared group of witches descended from the French practiced in rural Louisiana after the Acadians settled there."

"You may be onto something," Tess said.

"The order relied on their herbal medicines and other beneficial natural magic to win the favor of the other settlers."

"What else?"

"That's all it says."

"Darn. Is Bienville a French name?"

"I think. It seems to tie in, but that's all this book has."

"We'll have to try and find something else."

After poring over the books at hand for almost an hour, they found only frustration.

"We'll have to find more books on witches of that era," Tess said.

They found a reference librarian, who helped them go through microfilm files of other books under the witchcraft heading.

There weren't any books specifically devoted to Louisiana witchcraft in the seventeen or eighteen hundreds but they did find some cross references. Under the Works Progress Administration, a book called *Gumbo Ya Ya* had been written. According to a synopsis, the book contained information about Louisiana voodoo practices.

"That's not what we want," Tess said. "We're not interested in voodoo. We're interested in finding out about some black magicians that may have lived in Louisiana."

The librarian spent some more time cross referencing, and finally through a computer search, they located an obscure reference in a book called *Legends of the Bayou Country*. "This is a privately published book," explained the librarian, a slender, blond woman. "I'll have to request it through inter-library loan. Since it's from another state and we're in the holiday season, it may take me awhile to get it."

"We need it as soon as possible," Tess said.

"I'll order it, and I'll call you as soon as it comes in." They gave her both their phone numbers, then headed back out to the car.

"She could have Bran kill us all before that book comes in," Tess said as they walked outside.

"Maybe not."

"We know he's got Nathan. He's bound to come after us next."

"So we'll just have to watch out for him. What else can we do?"

"Move away?"

Casey put an arm around her shoulders. "Relax. Will you just relax? We're doing all we can."

"I know," Tess said. She kissed his cheek lightly. "I'm just scared."

"Me, too." Casey said. "Let's get out of here."

Bran watched the Buick pull away from the curb. He was standing in front of the courthouse across the street from the library, and he had been there for a long time, partially concealed by the shadows cast by the huge white columns in front of the building.

He had thought about hiding in the backseat of the Buick and waiting, but he'd decided against that.

He could be patient. He would get to them soon. Very soon. Then they'd be sorry they'd ever thought about casting spells on him.

"Do we just go on with business as usual?" Casey asked as Tess steered the Buick toward home.

"We have to, don't we?"

"Charisse knows we're suspicious."

"But if she thinks we're hiding and plotting against her, she might hurt S.W. Or she might try to kill us quicker. I think, until we've figured out exactly what she is and what she's after, we'd better try to stay cool."

"I think you're right."

They listened to the radio for awhile, and as they turned onto Tess's street, they were both beginning to feel a little calmer.

They'd even begun to talk about things other than magic. Then they spotted the police car parked in Tess's driveway. Tess almost ran the car onto the curb.

What could the cops want, unless someone had reported them being at the Bienville house.

That was all they needed now. If they got arrested, it would certainly alert Charisse, and that would sink them for sure.

Twenty-Three

Come Into My Parlor

Tess felt as if she were walking into an inquisition as she stepped through the front door. Casey was just behind her, but even that moral support wasn't comforting enough, not when she considered the possibility that they were going to be locked up together.

Her nerves were jumping as they trudged into the living room where a police officer was standing beside the Christmas tree, speaking with Mrs. Ryan.

Mrs. Ryan's face registered sudden surprise when she looked over and saw Tess.

"This is my daughter," she told the tall, blond-haired officer.

"Hello," the policeman said. He was wearing a blue uniform with a name tag that read Officer S. Williams.

"Hello," Tess said quietly, trying to prepare herself for an accusation.

"Officer Williams is trying to locate Nathan," Mrs. Ryan said. "His mother mentioned you as one of his friends."

"Yes," Tess said cautiously. How much could she afford to tell the officer?

If she or Casey mentioned Charisse and witchcraft, he'd think they were crazy. He'd probably haul them in for further questions. He might even think they were responsible for Nathan's disappearance. They couldn't let that happen.

With the two of them out of the way, Charisse would have a free reign to wreak whatever evil she desired.

Tess longed to reach for Casey's hand for comfort, but she didn't want the cop seeing that and misinterpreting it. She let her hands hang at her sides, and she looked the man directly in the eyes.

"When did you see your friend last?"

"I saw him the last day of school," Casey said. "He was going to stay late to use the computers. His at home is kind of old and slow."

"His mom says he never made it home. What about you, Miss Ryan?"

"A couple of days ago," she said. "I got sick."

"Your mother mentioned that."

She nodded slowly. Apparently her mother hadn't mentioned the sight of Nathan's head. It was just as well that didn't get on the cop's note pad, either. "Sometime before I got sick," Tess said.

"Did Nathan have anybody that didn't like him? Any enemies?"

Tess lifted her hand and bit her finger nervously. The obvious answer was Bran. She could give the cop his name. That might get him picked up for questioning. Maybe if he was out of the way for a couple of days, Casey and she would have some breathing room.

That might also tip their hand to Charisse, however. She didn't know what to do. She wanted to ask Casey, to talk it over with him, but there was no way to do that.

Finally she shrugged. "No one that I know of," she said. "No one special. He was kind of a scholarly guy. People always pick on people they think are nerds, you know."

"Yes ma'am. But you can't think of anyone that would wanted to hurt Nathan?"

She looked at Casey who gave her just the slightest hint of a nod.

"There's no one," she said.

"These aren't exactly the merriest of holidays are they?" Casey asked. They were walking through the crowd at the mall a couple of days after the visit with the policeman.

With all of the Christmas shoppers out and about, they felt safe in public. Bran was less likely to strike here, and Charisse also wouldn't want to do anything to them in front of witnesses. Being out helped lift some of the depression, which had set in as they'd sat around their homes.

It didn't take away the thoughts of Nathan, however. They found themselves wondering what he must have suffered. It was what everyone was talking about. On the local news, they had shown his picture and described what he was last seen wearing.

The newspaper also had printed his picture along with his vital statistics. Grimly, Tess thought that they were no longer accurate.

Parents were deeply concerned that a local boy was now a milk carton candidate, and speculations were on the lips of every cluster of kids they passed in the mall.

To many, Nathan was just the squirrelly little nerd who understood all of the equations in chemistry class and won all the computer games. But they were still upset by his disappearance. He was one of the faces in the hallway, one of the faces that wouldn't be there anymore.

If he had not disappeared on the last day of school before the holidays, the loss would probably be even more acute and noticeable.

Tess wished he was around. He'd always been her friend and he'd helped her through many a rough assignment.

She was losing all her friends in one way or another. Today she wished she were out with S.W. searching for a present for Casey That would have been fun. That would have been what she should have been doing.

"I can't really believe I was looking forward to this season," she said softly. She was pale, and her eyes had taken on a sunken look because she had not slept well since part of Nathan had put in an appearance under the tree.

She had spent a good deal of time reading, but with all of the information she had amassed, she didn't feel confident. She had not learned of any way to stop Charisse, and the book she wanted had not yet arrived at the library.

Vampires could be killed with a stake through the heart, werewolves with a silver bullet, but there were no easy answers about dealing with a sorceress and her henchman, or whatever Bran might be called, at least not in the books she'd read.

"Let's go look at the candy shop," Casey suggested.

"No," Tess said. "I don't like this."

"The mall?"

"No. We keep waiting for her to do something, but we don't even know what she wants!"

"Maybe she's just playing with us."

"She's playing rough. Poor Nathan. Who knows what she did to him? She might have fed him to her cat."

"Don't think of those things."

"And where has she got Bran?"

"He may be at home."

"I tried calling this morning. I was going to disguise my voice, but I didn't have to. His mother answered. She said he's not home. He left her a note that he'd be visiting some friends."

"She didn't seem worried?"

"She sounded drunk, or hungover, I guess. Kind of explains why he was so mean."

Casey slipped his hands into the pockets of his jeans. "Charisse is getting ready for something?"

"Maybe."

They continued to walk along, dodging people whose arms were filled with packages, people who were looking at hectic but at least normal holidays.

Tess was thinking about leaving when she spotted S.W. and Charisse moving along one of the side hallways. They had Serena Adamson with them. All were dressed in brightly-colored new outfits.

Charisse even looked more normal in a black skirt and black tights along with a green sweater.

Serena, a blond-haired girl with green eyes Tess envied, had been S.W's buddy in junior high. They had drifted apart in ninth grade though she had occasionally come along with Tess and S.W. to a movie or ball game over the last couple of years.

Tess grabbed Casey's arm, stopping him and nodding toward the trio.

"What's Serena doing with them?" he asked.

"They're recruiting from among familiar ranks."

"Recruiting."

117

"For their coven."

"Their what?"

"Their coven. It's a group of practitioners. I've been reading about it. That's what she has to be doing, forming a group or some kind of magic circle."

Looping her arm casually around Casey's, she started dragging him forward.

"What are you doing?" he asked.

"We're going to casually bump into them," Tess said. Casey stumbled along beside her, trying to look nonchalant. S.W. and the others were coming out of a card shop, so Tess pretended that was where she and Casey were headed, angling toward the doorway and acting as if she wasn't paying close attention to the others.

She tried to make her sideward glance seem natural, and then she faked an expression of surprise.

S.W. looked back with a similar face. "What are you two up to?" she asked, sweetly.

"Just picking up some cards," Tess said, nodding politely. "Serena, Charisse."

"Christmas shopping never ends," Casey added, with an effort to match Tess's performance.

"What are you guys doing?"

"We're planning a party," Serena said, holding up a bag which seemed to be filled with crepe paper and other items.

"A Christmas party?" Tess asked.

"No, everybody goes to Nancy's. We're planning a New Year's Eve party," Serena said brightly. "The New Year isn't far away, and S.W. suggested it since we haven't had much time to spend together in a while."

"There are several New Year's parties every year, but we're hoping ours will be the most popular," S.W. said.

Tess bit the inside of her lip. She could understand why they'd roped Serena in now. She was popular, and her mother was on the city council. Other parents respected her, so a party involving her would be well attended even when parents might veto other gatherings where they feared liquor would be too plentiful.

That must be what Charisse wanted. To get everybody together. Not at a party like Nancy's, but at a party on her turf where she was in control. But why? What was she up to?

"Where are you guys having your party?" Casey asked.

"My house," Charisse said. "We're going to fix the place up.

That news hit Tess hard. Charisse would be trying to lure all the kids into her lair.

Come into my parlor…

Twenty-Four

Caroling

Tess's heart was not in it as she dressed for Nancy's party She left her new hat dangling over the corner of her mirror and didn't spend much time on her hair.

She was more worried about what might happen than how she looked. Even though Charisse was obviously planning something big for New Year's, she might not mind having Tess and Casey out of the way before then.

That meant caution would be essential tonight even though Tess refused to let potential danger keep her away from the party It wasn't that she wanted to attend that badly, but she wanted to be on hand to keep an eye on activities.

If Charisse tried to knock her off in front of the crowd, it might go a long way toward convincing S.W. and everyone else of the danger — Tess knew she couldn't convince them otherwise.

They'd only laugh if she told them Charisse was a sorceress and that she was planning something incredibly evil at her New Year's Eve party Then they would just waltz in like lambs to the slaughter.

She had to bide her time, wait for an opening that would allow her to stop Charisse. She buttoned on a paisley vest and selected her black blazer to wear with her jeans, wound a loose scarf around her neck, and went down to wait for Casey.

He arrived a little before seven. Her father didn't hide his disapproval this time as he looked over Casey's dark jacket and torn jeans. If only her dad could understand the things that really mattered.

After a brief conversation with her parents, she followed Casey out to The Judge.

"Ready?" he asked.

"As I'll ever be."

At Nancy's, Christmas music played on the stereo, and the living room was already filled with kids when Tess and Casey arrived.

Nancy greeted them at the door, a broad smile spreading across her features. Her wavy, dark brown hair was pulled back into a ponytail, and she was wearing a new red dress and black stockings.

"How are you?" she asked graciously as she ushered them into the foyer. Her family lived in a large, ranch-style home, and she seemed to be in training to become a suburban hostess in her own right as soon as she was old enough to marry someone of equal social standing.

That was probably why her family bankrolled her annual soirées, Tess speculated. They wanted to make sure she was up to the social demands of domestic bliss.

"You guys want eggnog?" Nancy asked after she'd helped them hang their jackets in the hall closet. "Or Cokes? Sprite?"

"Nothing for now," Tess said with a forced smile. "We'll just mingle."

"Okay."

Nancy flashed an awkward smile at Casey and moved on into the living room to chatter with a couple of kids who were a bit more firmly entrenched with the in-crowd.

"I don't think she likes me," Casey said.

"There's not a lot of room in Nancy's world for 'different,'" Tess said. "Don't let it bother you."

"I'll survive."

They found a couple of friends—Gerda Martin and Jere Walker— who had staked out a corner, so they lingered, talking about nothing in particular for a while.

Tess was almost beginning to feel she could unwind and enjoy the evening when she looked up and saw Nancy pushing her way to the center of the living room.

"Can I have everyone's attention?" she asked. As she spoke, Denny Wagner turned down the music.

Everyone began to turn, and Tess assumed it was time to get ready for the caroling excursion.

She felt her jaw drop when she realized that was only part of Nancy's purpose. The crowd had parted slightly so that everyone could look toward Nancy, and standing with her were Serena and Charisse. Tess noticed S.W. was also standing in the living room's arched entryway.

"I want everyone to meet a new friend," Nancy was saying as she put an arm politely around Charisse's shoulders.

"I'm afraid I almost slipped up and didn't invite her tonight, but Serena pointed out my oversight. This is Charisse Bienville who's new to Pembrook High this year."

Charisse gave an almost shy nod as she was presented to the crowd, bowing her head just slightly so that a lock of hair obscured a portion of her face. She looked hesitant and vulnerable, and that seemed to win everyone over.

Especially since she looked gorgeous in a tight-fitting black dress that had a hemline that was within a half-inch of embarrassing.

People began to say hello to her, and she politely nodded back.

"Everyone will want to welcome her," Nancy said. "Let's do it while we're getting our coats on because it's time to hit the streets. I'm sure the neighbors are waiting."

The party, after all, wasn't designed just to keep Nancy popular. It was also arranged so that the neighbors were impressed as well.

This year the event had a threefold purpose, Tess decided. It was also winning everyone over to Charisse. She watched as Charisse whispered to Nancy.

The remark prompted Nancy to raise her hand. "I almost forgot," she said. "Charisse is planning a big New Year's Eve bash, so all of you should start making plans to be there. Serena and S.W. are helping out, and it's going to be a great way to ring in the New Year."

That drew an enthusiastic round of applause from the group. "It's getting worse," Casey whispered.

"It's what she's planned all along," Tess said. "We haven't seen it because we've been so preoccupied with Bran and everything."

"You think she's roping everybody into her circle? Is that her plan?"

"I don't know. Let's hope that darned book gets here soon."

They watched people begin to file into the hallway for their coats, and eventually they followed, collecting their coats and joining the others on the front lawn, where Nancy was distributing little photocopied booklets of carols.

"We'll make our way through the neighborhood," she said. "Just like always."

"You think we're safe?" Casey asked quietly.

"We'll see," Tess said.

The cluster of teenagers set off along the sidewalk, huddled into a unit as a crisp night wind whipped at them. The temperature seemed to be dropping, and Tess was beginning to wish she *had* worn her hat after all.

She was thankful when Casey put an arm around her. The gesture was comforting as well as warming.

She let some of her weight rest against him as the group moved up the driveway of the first house on the route. Maybe she was a little woozy. Maybe some of her sickness hadn't left her. Placing a hand against her face, she realized her skin was warm.

Her immediate instinct was to glance toward Charisse. She jerked her head so quickly that she caught the girl staring at her. At first Charisse seemed about to look away, but instead, she gave Tess a knowing smile.

"She's doing something to me," Tess tried to whisper to Casey, but her voice was too weak to make him hear.

She leaned against him for support and tried to keep an eye on the red-haired girl as they stopped at the doorstep.

Nancy ran up and rang the bell, and when a man and his wife came to the door, the group began to sing "God Rest Ye Merry Gentlemen."

Tess watched Charisse. She wasn't singing. She was just standing with her booklet held in front of her, going through the motions.

Struggling to keep her head up, Tess began to sing, forming words as carefully as she could. Some of the ill feeling subsided as the tunes continued, and by the time they had finished and were ready to move on to another house, she had regained some of her strength.

"What's she doing?" Casey asked.

"I don't know. Just watch her. We'll figure out what she wants."

They stopped at another house and sang a new set of carols including a rendition of "Jingle Bells" and "Silent Night" The family, which included several young children, applauded when the tunes were finished, and then the group moved on, heading along toward the old Renwick house which was next in their curved route.

The ancient oak trees along the street made the area shadowy, and Tess slid her arm around Casey's back as they entered the darkened stretch.

She could sense something coming.

As the others laughed and talked, she began to look around. There were plenty of trees here, plenty of hiding places.

"Something's about to happen," she warned Casey. "I just sense it."

She saw Bran before anyone else did. At first, in the darkness, his white face seemed to be hovering in midair, but when he emerged from shadow, she could see the outline of his shoulders.

"Look out!" she shouted as Bran came forward.

"What does he want?" Bradley Evans asked.

"I thought he'd lost his head or something," someone else muttered.

Bran took a spot on the sidewalk in front of the group, his scowl as deep as ever.

His jacket and jeans were dirty, and a film of mud had dried over his heavy boots, all of it making him look like some kind of wild man.

Everyone seemed to be frozen as he lowered his head like a wolf surveying his prey.

Tess watched his eyes as they moved slowly about in their sockets. He was looking for something.

For her!

She realized it as her gaze locked on her. There were a couple of people between her and Bran, but he picked her out of the crowd.

Tess's hand tightened around Casey's arm as the fear seized her, and she realized Bran would probably be after Casey, also. They were both in trouble.

A sputter of terror began to issue from the crowd, and as Bran came forward, kids began to dart out of his way.

Jere tried to say something to him, but Bran elbowed him aside. That angered Richie Mathers, who was on the football squad, and he tried to rush toward Bran.

Bran sidestepped him expertly and then angled a hard elbow back into the boy's face. An ugly crunching sound followed as Richie's nose was crushed back against his skull.

Richie's hands moved quickly to the wound, and he went stumbling backward, off balance. Blood seemed to be spraying through his fingers as he tumbled to the ground while letting out a loud moan.

Casey tried to get in front of Tess to protect her, but Bran grabbed the lapel of Casey's jacket and dragged him forward, slamming a fist into his stomach. Casey doubled over, gurgling as bile rose in his throat.

Tess wanted to help him as he crumpled to the sidewalk, but Bran was headed right toward her, his hands raised for her throat.

She could see his thumbs bending, preparing to crush her windpipe once his fingers went around her neck. She turned to run but somehow managed to get her feet tangled around Casey's legs.

Pain fired through her knees as they struck the pavement, making it difficult for her to scramble away even as she heard Bran's boots pounding toward her.

She tried to pull herself along but managed to move only a couple of inches, and then she felt his tug at her jacket. He'd grabbed her coattail and was about to drag her back toward him.

Balling her hands into fists, she prepared to pound at him. She would struggle and claw at his eyes. He wasn't going to get her without a fight.

As she felt herself being twisted around, she heard gasps from her scattered friends.

"Somebody do something," Nancy screamed. "He's gone really crazy!"

Now Tess was facing Bran, and his face seemed demonic. His eyes were filled with rage, and his grimace pulled his lips back revealing his teeth.

Tess began to pound her fists against his chest and shoulders even though her head was swimming worse than it had been before. Her fear was pumping adrenalin into her brain, giving her new strength.

Even that wasn't enough.

125

His hands moved toward her throat. What could she do? Casey was still stunned. Everyone else was too frightened.

She was about to scream when the softly spoken words seemed to come from nowhere.

"Bran."

The sound his name made Bran hesitate.

"Bran, what are you doing?"

He turned around, seeming confused.

"There's no need to hurt anybody."

Tess felt almost as surprised as Bran.

It was Charisse talking, telling Bran to step back and leave Tess alone. He obeyed …

Twenty-Five

Enemies

"It was a setup to make her look good," Tess complained the next day as she and Casey sat in a booth at the Petite Burger.

"She's gained total control over Bran," he agreed.

"And everybody thinks she's *super* now that she's rescued me, even if Bran did manage to disappear again before anybody could get the police." Tess slammed her fist down on the table. "She planned the whole thing, even had a spell to keep me half-dazed so I couldn't run well. Now no one will believe she's dangerous. Everybody will go to her party, and then there's no telling what will happen."

"Calm down," Casey said, reaching across the table to pat her hand. "We're going to find a way to stop her."

"We can't even get the book we need at the library, and it's almost Christmas. By New Year's she'll have a stack of corpses, piled on top of poor Nathan's."

Casey could only nod in agreement. "She's been setting us up all along," he said. "Maybe we need to get a priest or something."

"I doubt even a priest would believe us." She bit down on the straw in her milkshake and sipped.

She was almost getting her pulse rate under control when the restaurant's door swung open, and a crowd began to filter in—S.W., Serena, Nancy, several other girls and, of course, Charisse. They were all laughing and giggling.

When they saw Tess, they waved and smiled, all except Charisse. She gave Tess a knowing smirk that conveyed all her smugness. She had everything under control, and she wanted to make sure Tess knew it.

The holiday season marched onward. More and more brightly-colored lights began to dapple houses and lawns, and the radio stations began playing festive music almost exclusively.

Tess helped her mom wrap packages for their relatives and for her dad, but she couldn't summon any real enthusiasm or Christmas spirit.

Her melancholy began to deepen so much that her mother became concerned about her and began taking her temperature at regular intervals, fearing that some vestige of her illness had lingered.

Tess tried to convince her nothing was wrong, but her mother kept asking questions, wondering where S.W. had gone and what was the matter.

"Have you just forgotten about all your friends because Casey has come along?" her mother asked. "You hardly hang out with the girls anymore. He's not the center of the universe."

"I realize that, Mom. He's just a friend!"

"You know you've got college just around the corner. Is it wise to get so involved with him? I'd hate for you to make any…mistakes."

The word was so heavy and severe it infuriated Tess. That was the last thing her mother needed to be worried about right now

"We won't, Mom. Don't try to tell me not to see him. I need Casey right now."

"Oh?"

"As a friend."

"Can't you do *anything* without him?"

"Just get off it," Tess said, leaving the room.

"Don't get angry. I'm trying to reason with you."

Tess wanted to scream, but she forced herself to turn around. "You don't have anything to worry about with Casey," she promised. "A lot of my friendships are in transition right now. That's all."

Her mother seemed to remain suspicious, but she allowed Tess to change the subject. At least that was a relief.

Tess didn't need tension with her mom on top of everything else. Why couldn't parents understand that if you had a situation to deal with, you didn't need them adding another form of friction? Maybe parents didn't realize how much they could mess with their children's minds.

The conflict forced Tess to avoid calling Casey because she didn't want her mother chastising her for being obsessed with him. She'd listened to her mom's lectures during previous relationships, and she knew how her mom's mind worked.

She wanted to tell her: "You don't have to worry about me getting too serious with Casey, Mom. You have to worry about me being killed by a sorceress!"

That would go over marvelously, no doubt.

Too bad it was the truth.

Tess was surprised in mid-afternoon when she received a call, not from Casey, but from S.W.

"Are you looking forward to Christmas?" S.W. asked. She sounded like the friend Tess had always known.

"It's okay," she replied.

"Did you get Casey something?"

"We haven't really thought about presents."

"I haven't even thought about Christmas the last couple of days. We've been so busy with the New Year's party. It's really getting hectic. Everybody's coming, you know."

"Oh really?" Tess asked.

"Yeah. We're getting RSVP's right and left. Everybody wants some to way to unwind after Christmas and before we have to go back to school."

And everybody's scared to get out on the streets because of Bran, Tess thought. They think they'll be safe in that big old house but they're wrong!

She kept those thoughts to herself, nervously twisting a lock of her hair with one hand.

"I hope you're going to come," S.W. said. "You really ought to be there."

Tess almost wanted to laugh. Of course she had to come. Charisse probably wanted her there most of all. She was the one Charisse hadn't been able to win over, so she probably had to be terminated, or killed, or whatever the polite term for it was.

She closed her eyes, picturing herself strapped down to some hideous stone altar while Charisse raised a sharp dagger over her. What a way to celebrate a new year.

"I'll be there," she said with more conviction than she actually felt.

Inside she was quivering. It felt strange to hear from her friend and to know that S.W. was trying to trick her.

Why did Tess have to be the one who realized what was going on? That was the hard job. She didn't like being the odd person out, the one who had to stand against the crowd.

All of her friends were suddenly enemies. She had not previously considered the conflict in these terms.

People she had once cared about were now planning to hurt her. Why should she go in and let herself get hurt just to try and free them from Charisse's hold?

Maybe she should just sit home and watch the New Year rung in on TV with Casey, and after they were all finished off or were forever bound to Charisse and her dark forces, she could take smug satisfaction in being the one who didn't follow the crowd.

The last one standing had the last laugh.

————

A few days before Christmas, Casey came over in The Judge, and with her parents reluctant consent, Tess went out with him for a drive. Her orders were to return in time for dinner because she had aunts and uncles and cousins who were beginning to arrive for the holidays, and Tess was expected to join in the usual rituals.

Getting out of the house crowded with relatives was like receiving a parole. She kissed Casey quickly after he'd opened the door for her, and then she slipped into the front seat.

"Where would you like to go?"

"Anywhere, just drive."

"I have some good news," he said.

"Good news? These days?"

"Really."

He walked quickly around the car, slid into his seat behind the wheel and pulled a book that was tucked under the front seat.

"I didn't get you a present," Tess confessed, but then she got a better look at what he was holding. It wasn't a present.

It was a small, worn paperback reinforced with a covering of clear plastic.

"The library called this afternoon," he said. "They just got it in, and they gave me a chance to pick it up before they closed."

Tess almost shrieked as she leaned over and hugged him.

The book could make a difference. They might have a better chance of understanding Charisse. They might find a way of defeating her.

"Why didn't you tell me on the phone?"

"I didn't know who might be listening. I figured it was better to show it to you."

"Have you looked at it?"

"Chapter Seven. It talks about the outlaw magic of the Louisiana Purchase."

"You're kidding."

"Only slightly."

Tess began to thumb through the book as Casey backed the car out of the driveway. As he had promised, Chapter Seven seemed to be the correct chapter.

"They moved into an area populated by outlaws?"

"A lot of outlaws from what I understand," Casey said. "There was time when the various governments disputed ownership of the region. They designated this stretch of land off limits to civil authorities and military authorities. All governments agreed to stay out of it. It stretched from Louisiana all the way to Texas, and the result was that all of these outlaws moved in there."

"I see that," Tess said, leaning forward and skimming the pages in the faint light from the radio's face on the dash. Reading was difficult, but she squinted to make out the lines.

"The magic circle went there also," she said.

"Fleeing persecution," Casey said. "They set up residence and practiced herbal medicine for the outlaws, a benevolent front. They practiced black magic for themselves."

The car cruised past a lawn which almost seemed to be ablaze with bright lights. A rainbow of colors flooded the front seat, but Tess didn't look up from the page.

"It says here the outlaws befriended them for a while?"

"Read on," Casey said.

Tess tilted the book more toward the dim light and scanned the next few paragraphs.

"They continued to practice their rituals. 'Practices which included animal sacrifices,'" she read, then flipped a page. "'Some scholars believe their practices may have gone beyond animal sacrifice. They endeavored to manipulate all the forces of heaven and earth.'"

"The outlaws got scared of them, and they decided they had to drive them out," Casey said.

Tess read more aloud. "'The massacre is recorded in some family histories. Taking arms, the outlaws went to war. They used fire.'"

Her voice cracked, and she had to stop.

"They killed them?"

"Something happened. In Louisiana, remember Nathan had mentioned something about Louisiana? Maybe they really were practicing black magic. They couldn't have deserved what happened to them. They got all of the group except one young girl. She was taken in by a man and wife who fled the region and traveled to New Orleans."

"The family name—"

"Was Bienville," Tess said, cutting him off "Which means Charisse is either the descendant of that child…"

"Or she's the same girl. You can see how that history would affect her disposition."

Tess closed the book and leaned back in her seat as the car moved under the town water tower, aglow with the strings of multicolored lights.

Charisse's home was only a couple of blocks away, but she didn't even look up the street. She didn't want to see the eerie old house. She was too frightened.

"What does she want here, and why now?"

"I don't know," Casey said. "But she obviously thinks we're her enemies."

Hampton was a town seventy miles east of Pembrook, a smaller bump in the road than Pembrook. Before she left the next day, Tess told her mother she and Casey would be asking in a matinee and going for pizza afterward.

That bought her some time. She hoped it would be enough as she slid into her seat in The Judge.

"You set?" Casey asked.

"Yeah, let's roll."

He gave the wheel a hard turn, and the car angled away from the curb with a lurch.

"One of these days I need to get this engine worked on," Casey noted.

"Later," Tess said. "Worry about it later."

"Right." He shoved his foot down on the gas and headed out toward the highway.

He'd come up with the idea for the trip. It was not a fun jaunt. They'd spent an hour at the library thumbing books and checking indexes and bibliographies, seeking out the nearest expert they could locate.

Many of the magic books were so old, the authors were long gone, and they were beginning to decide there was nothing to be found when a new reference librarian began to talk to them.

Tess explained what she wanted, and the woman's face brightened.

"I know someone who might have information on American magic," she said. "There was a girl in here a few weeks ago."

"Oh?"

"I say a girl. She was in her twenties. She's working on a book about witches, and she's been traveling all over. She's around Pembrook trying to find out if there were witches here."

"You're kidding," Casey had exclaimed.

"No, no. She talked to me quite a while. She has a degree in folklore, but she hasn't been having any luck finding a teaching position, so she's working on a novel called *Witchdance*."

"That's almost a miracle," Tess said under her breath.

"A miracle?"

"Well, after the holidays, I have to finish a paper on this stuff, and I need some help," Tess said.

After obtaining a name and phone number, they went to Tess's home and put in a telephone call, then planned their trip to meet Felice Wharton.

The drive took a little longer in The Judge than it would have in just about any other vehicle Tess could imagine, but by mid-afternoon they were pulling into the driveway of the little rented house where Felice was staying.

Tess noticed an old Volkswagen Beetle parked in the driveway and decided that if she didn't have any helpful information, at least Casey could swap car repair stories with her.

Even after seeing the car, Tess wasn't quite prepared for the sight of Felice.

She was a tall, thin girl with waist-length hair that was dark and wavy, and she wore a loose-fitting dress along with white socks and tennis shoes. Her glasses had blue frames, she wore no makeup, and, in spite of all that, she was one of the most attractive girls Tess had ever set eyes on—even with the dark, serious mood she seemed determined to present.

"So ya think you've found ah real witch?" she asked. Her voice was thick and deep, the accent down-home Southern.

"Throws you a little, dudden it?" she said, recognizing Tess's expression.

"A little."

"I try to weed a little of it out on the phone. Never know when it's an agent or a publisher callin'. I don't like to sound too stupid and most people tend to think Southern is stupid. Funny, no other regional accent gets that rap, but then that's another dissertation."

"Are you from Louisiana?" Casey asked.

"Sorry. Alabama. Ever hear of Mobile?"

"Once."

"Come on inside," she said. She ushered them into the small front room of her house. The sitting area was neatly arranged with a glass-topped coffee table as the center piece, but tucked in one corner was a rolltop desk.

A laptop computer was set up there and beside it a printer. Books were stacked beside the computer as well as on the floor.

"So what is it you need to know? You came a long way just to talk to some silly girl working on a book," Felice asked.

"But you're familiar with magic and folklore?" Casey asked.

"Somewhat," she said.

"Then you know about the Louisiana Purchase massacre."

She smiled. You've done some deep research. There's not much said about that. That whole badlands area is all but forgotten, and there's hardly any reference in oral tradition or written record about the killings of witches or black magicians. There was a lot of other violence in that area including family and ethnic clashes so it's almost lost."

"But you're familiar with the legend?" Tess asked. "I've done a good bit of research, yes."

"Well what do you think?"

"I guess it's like Salem. The people thought they had a group of witches on their hands, and they took action, employed fire. An element. Fear and superstition motivate people to do crazy, awful things."

"What if they were real? What if they were practicing evil magic?" Tess asked.

"That's a long shot. Louisiana had a lot of voodoo practitioners in rural areas even up into the 20th century, but I've never really figured the witches of the legend were real. Those who really traffic in the black arts, if you will, are pretty rare. You understand, there are a lot of varieties of magic practitioners."

"And all magic has its good and its bad side, right? For Santeria there's Brujeria. For Merlin there's Morgan le Fay. I've read some," Tess said. "I'm not worried about people who practice neo-pagan rituals. We're talking about something more than ceremonies at the autumnal equinox."

"Interesting you mention Morgan le Fay. Her name, Fay, suggests a role, as magician or possibly a spiritual or supernatural being. On the dark side, one school of thought is that they were demoted angels, not quite demons but with ties to the Devil. "

"Whatever they are, we think the Bienville story is true," Tess said. "That one practitioner survived. We think we know her. If she wasn't a magician practicing black magic then, she is now. Or if she's something like you suggest..."

That raised Felice's eyebrows. "You've got to be kidding," she said, a broad grin crossing her features. "Somebody sent you over here to pull my leg."

"No. We're deadly serious."

She fixed them tea as they began their story. They moved the party into the kitchen where they sat around her small table and laid out their suspicions, detail for detail.

Felice settled back in her chair when they were finished and let out a whistle. "Figured y'all would expect that reaction," she said. "Have to live up to the stereotype. Now then, about your friend. Sounds a whole lot like she'd read up on this stuff even more than you have. I'd tend to believe your first inclination was the correct one. She's probably doing all this to get some friends together. She could be just a lonely girl."

"We've asked ourselves about that," Tess said. "But the cat, Bran, Nathan, the reaction with S.W., and all the—"

"You could be reading a lot into everything," Felice said. "Sounds like Bran was pretty crazy to begin with. This all started because you thought she was a real magician of some kind, maybe she just decided to play along. Heck, she's got the whole student body comin' to her party. It's working."

"You say she's read up on it," Casey said. "That means what she'd doing is accurate? For black magic? Dark sorcery?"

"True *maleficium*? It's rare, but it sounds it when I hear it second hand, yes. Some of it matches with what I understand of black magic practices, some of the most ancient ones, but you have to understand—"

"The Bienville Witch," Tess persisted. "What they dubbed the one who fled the neutral strip. She could still be alive?"

"If she practiced real black magic? I suppose, theoretically she could have found a way to make herself immortal if she wasn't already some kind of magical being. That's one of the legends of black magic's goals, but I just don't think you've got that big a problem. Remember, I study this from an academic perspective. I am essentially an academic—even if that sounds pretentious. I've studied this from a viewpoint of what people believe. Superstition is a big part of a lot of it, and that's led to some awful things. Probably what happened in the neutral strip was superstition gone crazy, not outlaws battling real magicians."

"If she is the Bienville Witch, or really an ancient sorceress, what would she be after? What would she want to accomplish."

"Could be a lot of things. Revenge, though it's been a long time. From what you tell me about her drawing your friends in, it sounds like she's trying to get a group of followers together. If she is real, she might have picked this time because of some cosmic alignment she's been waiting for, for a grab at some kind of ultimate power."

Tess gripped the edge of the table. "That's what I've been afraid of."

"I'll give you this for another coincidence," Felice said. "Don't get me wrong. I'm still skeptical, but I've been studying this area. The group that moved to Louisiana. They're supposed to have been from around here. If she wanted to reestablish her group, she might want to come back to where it all started."

Twenty-Six

The Party Begins

Christmas offered no joy or merriment. Tess endured the festivities, trying to smile as her relatives laughed and the younger family members played with their toys, but even with the tinsel and brightly-colored paper, her mood remained gray.

She found herself drawn to the window where she watched winter clouds crawling across the sky. The days now seemed to pass like those clouds—slowly dragging along but headed for a storm.

She talked to Casey on the telephone, and in their conversations they racked their brains to come up with ways to head off the party. Nothing seemed to work.

The buzz was that everybody would be going. After all, with Bran on the loose somewhere and Nathan missing, parents favored a nice safe party at someone's house.

Tess thought about making phone calls, but that seemed pointless. Who would believe her?

The only choice she had was to go to the party and try somehow to expose Charisse without looking like some horrible, superstitious maniac. What a nightmare!

She wished something like a vial of holy water or some other symbol might be used, but there were no guarantees.

Although her experience was primarily with folklore and not black magic, Felice had tried to help in finding some effective weapons.

What she had learned in her research was not much beyond what Tess had determined, however. There were only speculations. Real black magic practitioners were apparently so rare no one knew how to handle them, though they seemed susceptible to the same damage human beings suffered. Weren't they human first, after all?

As Christmas Day passed and the final days until the party flipped by, Tess and Casey made plans, frequently calling Felice for pointers. Incessantly plowing through library books and more websites, they decided that at some point Charisse would make a move at the party. She would do something to reveal her power and thus make her attractive to the other kids. Why else would she be getting everybody together? She wanted a vast source of energy.

Once she made her move, Tess and Casey would act before she had a chance to win converts—if that was indeed her purpose. They would capture her if possible. If necessary, they would find a way to destroy her.

From everything Tess understood in her research and discussions with Felice, those who tried to turn magic to evil ends were vulnerable to the elements—fire, earth, and water.

Since they manipulated nature with their evil magic, perhaps that made them equally susceptible to nature.

That was probably what prompted such references in even humorous stories such as *The Wizard of Oz*, but, unfortunately, Tess didn't expect Charisse to melt if splashed with water.

Fire had worked in the hideous massacre of Charisse's friends. The thought of that was awful, terrifying.

Tess wasn't sure what it would take, but she and Casey decided they would be ready.

They purchased disposable lighters, plenty of them, and selected loose-fitting clothes for the party so that they could conceal the weapons. Torching the place would be a last resort, but Tess reasoned that the splintering old wood of the house would burn well if it came to that.

For Charisse, the countdown to the New Year was more exciting. She felt empowered by the encouragement from S.W. and Serena, especially when they joined her in the preparatory ceremonies.

In the basement, they lit the candles and dripped samples of their blood into the Chalice of Eden she had saved. She remembered the first ceremony from so many years ago when she had joined the others, including Marie Bertiaux who had taught them the ancient ways, from the old country and before.

Now they were reawakening the old, making it new again. Slowly, Charisse taught the chants, then the ceremonial movements.

"Is it going like you wanted?" S.W. asked once they had completed their requests to the dark forces. "You know people are still talking about Nathan's disappearance. They're worried. What if people don't come? What if they don't join us?"

"There's nothing to worry about. Nothing," Charisse reassured. "The kids will come, and they'll see how strong we are, and they'll want to join us."

Working in unison was wonderful again after so many years without sisters. Soon the glory of those long-ago days would be restored.

Before the massacre, the group's magic had been growing, becoming stronger. If only they had been allowed to flourish, then they might have claimed the throne of the universe as Marie had hoped.

With a cluster of young members around her, Charisse might again aspire to that expectation. She might become the most powerful sorceress alive. The cosmic forces would be perfect at the stroke of midnight on New Year's morn. A circle birthed on that hour would become a force to behold, and she would sit at its head …

She laughed as she sat in her old armchair again. Soon she would have a more worthy throne.

New Year's Eve began as a gray day, and as the hours passed, the temperature began to dip. By evening, the weather was chilling.

"I guess you'll need to bundle up good for the party," Mrs. Ryan said as Tess began to get ready.

"Sure, Mom," she said as she tugged on a dark sweater which matched the gray slacks she was wearing. She'd already stuffed lighters into the pockets, and she had more in the pockets of her parka.

She paced in her room while she waited on Casey to arrive, and she watched the seconds flash by on the face of her clock radio. Midnight would come soon, and she couldn't help remembering that midnight was designated as the witching hour.

Casey was wearing his black coat as well as a black floppy-brimmed hat. After tipping it to Tess, he showed her the matches secreted in the band.

"A backup," he explained.

"We may need it," Tess said.

The party was already in full swing when Casey wheeled The Judge onto Charisse's street. Her driveway was lined with cars, and other vehicles were parked on the shoulder of the road.

"Looks like everybody's here," Tess said.

"Everybody who's anybody," Casey agreed. He pulled the car slowly onto the shoulder of the road. "I see Jere's car, and Jack Cook's."

"There's Tracy Ellen's Porsche," Tess added, Casey killed the engine. "Ready?"

"As I'll ever be."

They climbed out of the car and walked slowly, almost hesitantly across the front lawn. S.W. answered the door when Casey knocked. She was wearing a slinky black dress, and a new pair of dangling gold earrings which seemed to have arcane symbols incorporated into their design.

"So glad you two could make it," she said with only a hint of sarcasm.

"Wouldn't have missed it," Casey said.

"Has there been any word on Nathan?" asked S.W.

"None," Tess said as she turned her back to Casey and pulled her hair up from her coat collar.

Carefully he took Tess's coat and then shrugged off his own coat and hat and hung them over a chair that was already draped with other jackets, mufflers and overcoats. Tess felt awkward letting her parka go, but she was comforted by the lighters in the pockets of her slacks.

She slipped her hands in just to check as she looked around the room. It appeared quite different than it had on their previous visit. Things had been fixed up.

Some new lamps had been added, providing brighter light, and with decorations on the walls and along the banister, she almost felt she was in a different place. It didn't seem eerie and threatening at all.

Especially not with the music. Hot music was coming from all directions.

One side of the room had become a dance floor, and kids were twisting and swaying in abandon that suggested they had no sense of danger.

Taking Casey's hand, Tess moved on past them into the kitchen. It also was cleaner and more brightly lit, and a new-looking table had been set up there with an array of chips and vegetables, drinks and dips.

A couple of guys were sipping beers near the rear of the kitchen. They snickered when they saw Tess looking at them. She turned away.

"So far it looks just like any other New Year's Eve party," Casey whispered as they pretended to look over the foods.

"It's not midnight yet," Tess reminded. "Give her time to get things swinging."

Bran easily entered the old shed behind the house, knocking off the rusty old padlock with a rock. He knew what he was looking for. The ax leaned in a corner, partially hidden by cobwebs. He brushed them away.

Just as he had dreamed while curled in an old storage shed near the school, the ax was waiting for him.

Charisse hadn't lied to him. Not since she had started visiting his dreams. He hadn't understood at first, but now he was willing to continue doing her bidding, no matter how cloudy his thought became.

Hoisting the ax, he held the double-headed blade in front of his face, and as the metal gleamed in the beam of moonlight that filtered in through the shed window, he began to smile.

S.W. led Jere onto the dance floor, and as others joined in, even more of the living room floor was utilized. Some couples even began to move up the stairs, dancing on the steps and along the second floor.

"We're playing all the best stuff," Serena explained as Tess and Casey emerged from the kitchen, almost bumping into her.

"You've planned a great party," Tess lied, hoping that her smile didn't look as false as it felt.

"We tried," Serena said, swaying with the music.

Tess looked around for Charisse. She was worried that the witch was not in sight. That couldn't be a good sign.

"Do you see Charisse anywhere?" she asked Casey as soon as Serena moved on.

"No."

"She must be downstairs."

"That's frightening."

"We'd better try and find her."

"Maybe that's what she wants. For us to confront her in private."

"Could be, but who knows what she's got planned."

Slowly, they moved into the living room, pretending to dance as they worked their way through the crowd. No one seemed to pay much attention to them. They were just one more couple.

Tess was eyeing the door which would lead downstairs when S.W. popped into her view. She was still with Jere, guiding him along.

"Are you having a good time?" S.W. asked, shouting over the music.

"Sure," Tess said.

S.W. was here to keep an eye on her, and she had to smile and go along with it. A gloomy feeling seemed to settle over her.

They were going to have to wait for something to happen, something that would signal the beginning of the evil. She knew the evil was coming.

But why? What was Charisse trying to accomplish? Just a new magic circle?

The answer came tumbling from above … literally. The severed head toppled off Stephen Kelsey's shoulders, and plummeted down into the living room, spreading the crowd apart as it thudded to the carpet.

Screams and shouts followed as the people crushed back against the walls, huddling in horror. Tess looked up to the second floor where the headless body teetered, a lost staggering stump.

After a second, the body collapsed over the railing also, falling like a bag of broken plates to the floor.

Then Bran stepped forward, the still-bloody ax in his hands, as he looked over the crowd.

All around Tess kids continued to scream and sob, and she could feel their fear. Their trembling seemed to create ripples in the air.

Clutching Casey's hand, she managed to contain her own terror. Bran would have to be stopped if he was about to go on a rampage, but she suspected Charisse might have other plans.

Slowly, Bran edged along the upper floor, heading for the steps.

"Let's get out of here!" someone shouted, and the stampede for the door began.

Tess and Casey huddled together as kids thundered past them. They knew the effort to escape would be futile.

A second later, as kids still crushed past them, they heard the shouts of dismay from the foyer.

"It won't open," someone shouted.

"Force it!" came another distinct voice, and then there was just a hubbub of sound—more screams and shouts and whimpers.

"Is she going to rescue everybody and make it all wonderful?" Casey asked.

"I don't know," Tess said. "That would make everybody really impressed about now."

"They'd do whatever she wants."

Tess glanced toward the stairs where Bran was slowly making his way down the steps. Lighters weren't going to be much of a defense against the steel of his ax.

She was wondering how they were going to defend against his onslaught when the lights went out.

As the room plunged into blackness, the panic among the ranks increased. Tess could hear kids running into each other, and more screaming began.

She held tightly to Casey and tried to let her eyes adjust to the darkness. She wanted to know where Bran was and what he was doing.

She didn't have to wait long.

Before she could pull one of the lighters from her jeans, a flame ignited across the room. It was a small orange burst that calmed to a quick flicker, and the golden light illuminated Charisse's face.

She was standing near the wall, her head was partially covered by a black cloak and hood.

"She's got a costume for effect," Casey observed.

"Yeah," Tess agreed, watching Charisse as she touched the match she held to the wick of a thick white candle.

As the wick caught fire, Charisse hoisted the candle over her head, somehow casting light over the entire living room, even though its luminance should have stretched only a short distance.

"Calm down," Charisse demanded.

Her voice was so shrill and loud that it stopped all of the kids in their tracks in spite of their fear.

"You have nothing to be afraid of," Charisse promised.

"Why do they always say that?" Tess murmured.

"It calms people down," Casey observed.

"I want everyone to relax," Charisse said. "Bran is under control."

"What the hell is going on?" someone shouted.

"Give me a second," Charisse said with a wry smile. "And I'll tell you what the hell is going on."

Twenty-Seven

Sacrifices

"Y ou're all here tonight for a reason," Charisse said, moving through the group as people parted.

When she had reached the room's center, she lifted her candle high again, so that the flame cast light on the circle of people around her.

"You are here to make a decision."

As she spoke, Serena and S.W. moved toward her, taking their places on either side of her.

"That's a real unholy trinity," Casey observed.

"That's what I'm afraid of," Tess said.

"You can be one of two things," Charisse continued. "You can become a part of the circle that we are forming, joining my friends and me to create an order of true power, or you can stand against us. If you choose the latter, you will become sacrifices."

As if to punctuate her last remark, Bran lumbered into the center of the circle, his shoulders hunched slightly as he hoisted the ax.

"No one can escape without making a choice," Charisse said. "Why are you doing this?" Nancy asked.

"I am the last of my line," Charisse said. "My sisters were killed off in the last century, but now I am ready to reestablish my order."

"Why now?" someone asked.

Charisse smiled. "Because the cosmic forces are about to become aligned again as they were in the year my sisters died. At the stroke of midnight, the opening for a new age of power will begin."

"Why did you pick us?"

She smiled. "Why you? Because this is the town where my circle was formed even though we brought together magic from very distant lands. I have come back to the place of my circle's roots, before we traveled south looking for a place we would escape notice. I will re-create the circle, and I will take steps not to lose its power again."

"You used us," Tess said, squeezing Casey's hand for the feeling of strength it provided.

Charisse's grin was an evil, gloating look. "I had to have someone to open the door," she said. "I had to have an invitation among your ranks, and you, Tess have more ability than you realize."

"You dropped hints that you could help us fight Bran," Tess said. "Then you used us."

"I needed an ally to win new friends. For a time I thought it would be you, Tess, but your heart proved too pure. I should have recognized earlier you were not driven by your wants. Fortunately your friend's will was not as strong."

S,W. laughed. "Sorry, Tess. You were always a good friend, but you couldn't offer the power Charisse could promise. The last few days have been wonderful. She can give us anything we want. Anything."

Tess clenched her teeth. "The afternoon when we came to see you…"

"Was the afternoon I truly began," Charisse said. "That afternoon I took the messages you wrote and determined the nature of each heart."

"I guess mine was the weakest," S.W. said, snidely.

"You started out just demonstrating what you could do with Bran," Tess said. "Then you began to tempt S.W, and you got me out of the way for a couple of days so you could fully corrupt her."

"I did not corrupt. I invited. All of you opened yourselves when you agreed to participate in the first ceremony. You were told that you should not cast spells unless you were willing to accept the consequences. S.W. joined me willingly."

"What about Nathan?"

"He made the wrong choice."

"That's all you have to say? What did you do with him?"

"That's not important."

Kids began to turn toward Tess, their eyes quizzical. They were waiting to see what she would do, looking to her for an answer, not about Nathan but about what they should do.

Some of them were frightened, but in others she could see the glimmers of anticipation. They liked what they were hearing. They wanted the power. They could be rid of uncertainties and questions. They could have anything they wanted, and they liked that.

"What will it be?" Charisse asked. "Will you take this last opportunity to join me, or will you be the first sacrifice?"

"It can't be as easy as you're talking about," Tess said. "It's not right to play the game the way you're playing it. To use great power just for personal ends."

Charisse laughed. "Been reading some philosophy with your history?"

Bran stepped forward, taking a spot only a couple of feet away. He was unquestioning, unwavering, ready to do her bidding. He was an evil warrior in service to a dark queen.

The crowd members began to huddle together, hugging each other, trying to brace for what might happen. Tess looked for signs of support, but she saw only fear.

"I won't join you," Tess said. "I should have realized early on that it's wrong to try and manipulate other people for your own good. Getting Bran off our backs seemed like a noble cause, but where does it stop? You want more than just to stop a bully. You want to control everything, everyone."

Charisse laughed. "Is that so bad? My friends were destroyed. I only want to create a world where we'll be safe."

"By controlling the will of other people to give yourself everything you want? That's wrong."

"Wrong is in the eye and the belief of the beholder," Charisse said, tossing a nod in Tess's direction.

The gesture sent Bran forward, and before Tess could back away, he grabbed her arm, yanking her toward him.

She tried to pull away, but he managed to get his arm wrapped around her neck. She struggled against his grasp, but he was inhumanly strong.

She tried to cry out, but her voice caught in her throat.

"Let her go," Casey demanded. Before he could offer any assistance, Bran swung the ax handle, the end striking Casey just above the eye.

The blow cracked against his skull, and he went reeling, stumbling and staggering until he was completely off balance.

Tess felt tears spilling from her eyes as she watched him crumple to the floor. He didn't try to get up. He didn't even move.

"Tess has become the first sacrifice," Charisse said. "Who will be my first new circle member?"

"What's this all about?" Nancy asked.

Charisse curled her lips into a knowing smile. "It's about having whatever you want, about power and control."

Nancy's eyebrows curled slightly, reflecting her apprehension along with the tremble in her lips. She was holding her hands in front of her, wringing them absently, but she seemed intrigued by Charisse's offer.

She'd been well trained by her family to seek what she wanted, to go after prestige and position. Tess felt her heart sink as she considered what must be going through the girl's mind.

"You'll kill us if we don't join?"

"Why bother to find out?" Charisse said. "Tess has volunteered. Let her provide the innocent blood we need. No one else has to die."

"I don't know if it's such a good idea," Nancy said.

Charisse took a step toward her. "Where are your applications for college?"

Nancy seemed a little surprised. A frown formed on her brow. "My what?"

"Your applications. Where is it you want to go to school?"

"I'm trying to get into Yale, but things haven't worked out yet."

"They can. Easily. If that's what you really want, we can take care of it. You'll be in the perfect circles there. You'll meet all the right people."

"How?"

"We'll cast a spell to fulfill your desire."

Nancy shook her head. "I couldn't do it that way."

"Isn't Yale what you really want? Isn't it what your father wants? Isn't what he demands?"

"How do you know that?"

Charisse arched her eyebrows. "I know many things."

Tess tried to shout, to tell Nancy not to listen, but Bran's arm across her throat was choking her. She could feel blood pounding in her temples. She wanted to break Nancy's concentration and the strength of Charisse's seductive charm, but she couldn't.

"I can't do that," Nancy said. "I can't let you do that to Tess." The others were watching, stunned, frightened, unsure of what to do.

"Tess made her choice," Charisse said. "She could have joined us. She could have developed powers she isn't even aware of for me. She chose not to. That is not your concern."

Slowly, Nancy began to nod, and as she did, she moved forward, stepping just behind Charisse.

"Who else will come with me?" the witch asked.

Someone else began to move forward, but Tess couldn't be sure who it was. The loss of blood flow and oxygen was beginning to tax her brain. Her vision was clouding, and her head was getting heavier and heavier.

She tried to will herself to stay conscious, but she couldn't. She was blacking out, slipping into a deep, dark pit of nothingness.

Her head was throbbing as she came around. At first she thought she was already sealed inside a coffin, but slowly her eyes adjusted, and she realized she was staring up at the ceiling.

She was on the floor of the basement, lying flat on her back with her hands and feet securely bound. Jerking her head to one side, she realized she had been placed at the center of a chalk symbol.

All around her, she could see the feet of the crowd members. They were standing side by side. Had they all joined Charisse?

She tilted her head back slightly and got her answer. Only a few had joined her. Nancy and a couple of other girls and guys. They were standing close to Charisse and Bran. Several of the other teens were now bound at their wrists, as well.

Tess wanted to scream as she realized—they were waiting to be sacrifices as well, all those who had decided not to join the circle.

She felt a tight sadness in her throat. Maybe if she'd acted earlier, or if she'd realized what lay in store before ever becoming involved with Charisse she could have prevented some of this and saved a few lives.

She'd been stupid, stupid to let the cat attack her, stupid to let Charisse trick her in the first place. She'd also been a fool to believe she could come to the party and outwit the sorceress.

Her carefully placed weapons, her weapons of fire were not accessible now.

"Should we sacrifice Tess now, or should we take someone else?" Charisse asked. "We must appease the forces of darkness."

She scanned the eyes of her small group of followers, watching for a flicker of disloyalty, but they all seemed to be willing to go along with her. She had gained control of them quickly. Her magic was growing stronger.

"No," Charisse said at last. "I guess Tess should be the first. She is the purest of heart, the perfect sacrifice."

Touching Bran's shoulder, she led him toward the center of the symbol.

"Ready?" Charisse asked.

He nodded his head slightly. Tess squirmed and struggled against her bonds, but there seemed to be no way to free her hands.

She could feel her heartbeat pounding in her chest, and her lungs constricted as she watched him hoist the blade.

"Great forces of the night, I call on you," Charisse said, raising her hands over her head. "I call on you to receive this sacrifice of pure blood. Come and take this lamb, this innocent one filled with energy…"

Tess felt her eyes fill with tears as she watched light dance along the ax blade, candlelight. Candles were placed all around her.

If she could somehow tip one over…

She tilted her head back, looking through blurry tears at one of the candles a few inches from her head. If she could knock it over, she might distract Charisse, buy some time at least.

The fire might not rage out of control, but by tipping a candle she might be able to sever some hidden connection with the nether realms or whatever Charisse was contacting.

Rolling her shoulders against the hard concrete floor, Tess pushed herself backward, bringing her hands closer to the candle.

The maneuver distracted Charisse, and she looked down with an angry scowl.

"Stop her!" she commanded.

Before Tess could reach the candle, Bran placed his foot on her wrists, pinning them in place. He kept the ax raised, and when Charisse nodded toward him, he lifted it over his head.

"No," Tess protested. "No!"

Bran didn't listen, not to her command. His orders were already scripted. Charisse had sealed his fate the afternoon she'd conjured the first spell. She had placed him under her control and had set her plan into motion.

Tess wished she could undo that moment. That was hopeless. She couldn't even control this moment. She could only wait for the blade, and pray.

"Hold it right there!"

The loud voice boomed through the basement, echoing off corners almost like thunder.

Tess tried not to feel the relief, but she couldn't help herself. Even if this was only a temporary reprieve, she had hope again.

The voice was Casey's. She craned her neck to look through the row of legs, and she could see him standing on the stairs. He held one of the lighters in his hand, and the flame had been turned up to the maximum power.

An orange column shot up from his palm stretching almost six inches into the air. It looked like a blow torch.

"Back off," he said.

The kids lined up as sacrifices immediately obeyed, breaking the circle.

"Stay where you are!" Charisse shouted, but they didn't listen. They began to scatter to the four corners of the room, and that confused the would-be circle members. They also began to step back.

"That's good," Casey said, stepping off the bottom stair and starting across the room. He seemed to be walking on the ceiling from Tess's point of view.

"Get out of here," Casey commanded.

Some of the kids, with their hands still bound, began to move toward the stairs.

"Don't let them leave," Charisse commanded.

"Your hold isn't strong enough on them," Tess shouted, even as she watched S.W. grab for one of the guys as he departed.

Bran lifted his foot, making a move to try and obey.

Tess forced herself to action, pushing with her feet and urging herself to slide along the floor. Her fingers brushed the candle and knocked it over.

Wax spilled and spread, hardening immediately.

"Nooo!" Charisse protested, grabbing at the candle, but the flame was extinguished as the wick sank into the soft pulp. The symbol's parameter was broken.

Obviously that weakened some of Charisse's control. The kids began to move faster then, hurrying up the stairs. "You can't leave," Charisse protested.

"Yes, they can," Casey said. "You didn't quite get them converted to the dark side."

As the procession continued, only S.W., Nancy, and Serena remained at her side.

Charisse was enraged. Her face turned a bright scarlet, and she clenched her fists at her sides as Casey advanced, keeping the lighter in front of him.

"Don't make me hurt you," he said.

Even through her anger, Charisse laughed. "You can't hurt me with that. You think you can just burn someone of my power. The days of that possibility are gone."

With a jerk of her head, she sent Bran shambling toward Casey. He no longer seemed confused. He seemed ready to strike.

"Stay back," Casey warned, twisting his wrist and letting the bright flame sway from side to side.

Bran ignored that and swung the ax in a wide arc. The blade was aimed for Casey's head.

"Get down," Tess screamed. She had managed to pull herself into a sitting position, but she couldn't get her hands free. The bonds were too tight.

Casey obeyed, dipping at the waist. The blade missed him by inches, and he sank to one knee and jammed his arm forward.

153

The blaze from his lighter touched Bran's pantleg and almost immediately ignited the fabric. The flame began to lick up his leg, and he started a mad dance, hopping on one foot as he dropped the ax and began to swat at the flame.

Casey didn't wait to be a spectator. He tugged a fresh lighter from his pocket and charged across the room.

Charisse started toward him as well with her three remaining companions—Nancy, Serena, and S.W.—close behind, ready to attack. Casey dodged Charisse and ducked the others, then launched himself on a slide that carried him quickly to Tess's side.

"Let's get out of here," he shouted as he helped her free her hands.

Charisse had spun around by the time they were on their feet, preparing to dive for them. S.W., Serena, and Nancy backed her up.

Casey flicked at his lighter, but the wheel threw sparks without kindling a blaze.

"It's a dud," he said tossing it aside.

Frantically, Tess reached into her pocket for one of her lighters, but she discovered her lighters were gone.

"Too bad," Charisse said. "I found those already."

She stood near the center of the room with her hands on her hips now, and seemed confident again. Just behind her, Bran had succeeded in putting out his leg and was picking up his ax.

The others stood shoulder-to-shoulder with her, blocking any easy chance of exit.

"Looks like we can still proceed with our plans," Charisse said. "We still have two sacrifices."

Twenty-Eight

Four Minutes to Midnight

"Not so fast," Casey warned, and he yanked another lighter from his shoe.

The spin of the wheel worked this time, and he quickly adjusted the blaze so that he had an all-new torch.

"I'm still willing to bet you don't want any part of this flame even if you do handle a candle okay," he said.

Charisse shrank back from the blaze, lifted one arm protectively in front of her face, but she didn't seem truly fazed. "You can't really stop me with just one element." Taking Tess by the arm, Casey moved forward.

"We'll see, he said.

Charisse inched back a step. The move seemed to lessen the confidence of her friends, and Bran stood by like an empty suit of armor. He was no longer an individual. He was only something she commanded.

"Run," Tess screamed.

She and Casey bolted together, charging through the center of the line-up. The move took everyone by surprise, and they were knocked apart by the impact.

Tess and Casey kept running, heading for the steps as the others tried to get re-oriented. They took the stairs two at a time, and the boards rattled under their weight.

At the top, Tess shoved the door open. They charged through the front room and headed for the exit. It was open, the spell or illusion which had held it previously had apparently given way because Charisse's concentration was elsewhere.

Tess started toward it, her hand circled around Casey's wrist, leading the way. He was still a bit dazed from the ax handle blow, and she realized some of the tension might be catching up with him.

She could feel the cold wind from outside as they neared the exit, but just as she was about to head through, the heavy, oak door slammed shut.

Frantically she grabbed for the knob, tried turning it, but the effort didn't work. The latch would not budge.

"We're trapped!" she screamed, slamming her palms against the wood.

"No, we're not," Casey said. "We'll find a back way like we did before."

Turning, they moved back along the entry wall. Casey spotted their coats and quickly grabbed for his, and Tess took hers as well.

She felt the lighters in her pockets and was comforted. "Let's keep moving," Casey said, as he shoved his hat down on his head.

They headed through the kitchen and down a hallway. It was not a direction which they had traveled before, but it seemed better than waiting around for Charisse to come for them.

The hallway stretched only a few feet to a doorway. Casey grabbed the knob. The mechanism clicked. "It's open," he said, giving it a yank.

The headless body tumbled out almost striking him. He jerked back, colliding with Tess, but she put her hands forward, steadying him before he could slam into her.

"It's Nathan isn't it?" she said looking down at the floor. After so much trauma this evening, the realization seemed to lock in a numbing shock more than a new jolt of terror.

"It is," Casey agreed. His eyes closed, and he clenched his teeth. "Bran must've just stuffed the body here after he was finished with it."

Tess peered back into the narrow storeroom and saw an old canvas mailbag stuffed in a corner. It was one from the school office.

"He hid him in that and dragged him here. Probably in the dark."

She knelt beside the body, wishing there had been something she could have done.

"Poor Nathan."

She knew she should be up and running again, but she couldn't force herself away. She touched his shoulder even though she knew she should have been repulsed by the awful absence at his neck.

Something crinkled in his coat pocket as her hand brushed across it.

Her eyes widened, and she looked at Casey, who looked back in amazement.

"Bran must have gotten him at school," he said.

"And whatever Nathan was getting from his computer board might..."

Without further discussion, they tore at the pocket, yanking out the folded sheet of computer paper.

"Read it," Casey demanded.

Tess squinted in the shadows, trying to make out the letters.

"Here," Casey said, flicking on the lighter.

In the light from the flame, Tess began to read, quickly scanning the introduction from Father Alison. "Here's an answer I think holds true to the legends. Practitioners who called on the forces of darkness violated natural law and were thus obliged to the elements."

"That's what we already knew," Casey said.

"Wait. There's more. A magic user, even one who has obtained immortality, is susceptible to the elements—fire, earth, water. A single element, such as the water thrown on the witch in *The Wizard of Oz* would not be effective against a powerful enchantress, but a combination might serve to..."

"All three?"

"I think I know what we can do," Tess said.

"An interesting piece of information," Charisse said from behind them. "But you will not get to find out."

Casey jacked up the flame on his lighter. "We'll see what one will do."

He thrust the flame forward into her face before she could throw up her arms to protect herself. The surprise flare forced her backward, and Casey pushed forward, slamming into her with all his weight and knocking her to the floor.

As she tried to get up, he reached back for Tess's hand, and they headed along the hallway. In the kitchen, they tried another direction, heading toward the back of the house as fast as they could.

"We've got to hurry," Tess said.

"What do you want to try?"

"Let's just get outside, then I'll make my suggestions." They pushed into a back bedroom and saw beams of moonlight streaming in through a narrow window.

"Break it," Tess suggested.

Casey looked around for a second and spotted a chair. Handing her the lighter, he grabbed the seat and hurled it at the glass.

The panes shattered, leaving a gaping opening. Quickly, Casey unfurled his scarf, wrapped it around his forearm then raked his arm across the exposed glass, knocking it away so that an exit was possible.

An instant after they'd squeezed through, S.W.'s head appeared through the opening. "You won't get away!" she warned. "You don't have a chance."

A second later, Bran appeared at her side and started through the window after them.

Ignoring the warnings, Tess and Casey charged around the house, moving toward The Judge. Tess heard Bran's weight hit the ground, but she didn't let that frighten her.

She couldn't be afraid anymore. She had to concentrate on success. If she didn't, Charisse would achieve her goals. "What time is it?" she asked.

"Ten minutes to midnight," Casey said.

"We've got to hurry."

"Where are we going?"

"Up the block."

They reached the car and piled into the front seat.

"Where up the block?" Casey asked as he turned the ignition.

"To the water tower."

"Whatever you say."

He backed the car around and pressed the gas to the floor. Tess kept her hands against the dash to steady herself, and the car shot forward through the night.

"They're coming," Casey warned, looking into his rearview. "Who?"

"Charisse and Bran."

Tess looked through the back glass to see the witch and her consort rushing along the pavement.

"We want them to follow," she said.

"Fire, earth, and water?" Casey asked.

"We'll make it rain on her."

As they neared the end of the street, Casey let the car rumble over the curve, and he guided it across the grassy square of land which bordered the tower.

The wheels began to sink in the soft earth, but he pressed the gas a little harder and managed to keep the vehicle moving until he was at the base of the tower.

"Who goes up?" he asked.

They climbed out of the car and looked up at the multicolored strands of lights which still dangled from the structure. They seemed to reach up into the clouds.

"Never mind, I'll go," he said.

Climbing on top of the car, he reached up for the bottom rung of the metal ladder set into one of the tower's legs.

The rungs began a good distance from the ground to prevent just what he was trying, and he couldn't quite reach it.

"I'll help," Tess said, joining him on the car. She laced her fingers, and with a leg up, Casey connected.

"What do I do? Look for a valve?"

"Or whatever. There has to be a way to drain it doesn't there?"

"Let's hope."

She watched him start the climb, praying he would make it, praying they had a chance. After he'd traveled only a few feet, a burst of wind hit him. He struggled against the gust and lost his hat.

For a moment, Tess feared he was about to fall, but then he steadied himself and kept moving.

Charisse's hand fell on her shoulder before she realized someone was behind her. The witch had managed to approach silently, and she had somehow climbed onto the top of the car.

Before Tess could resist, Charisse grabbed a handful of her hair and yanked her forward. Tess tried to push her away, but a hand closed on her chin and forced her head back.

"You can't stop me. The clock is about to strike twelve."

As Tess struggled to free her throat from Charisse's grasp, she realized S.W. and Nancy were present as well, and they were helping Bran onto the ladder.

"No," she growled. "Not—"

"Yes. Your friend just lost hope."

Charisse forced Tess to turn her head and to look up as Bran began his ascent. One hand was still closed around an ax handle while he lifted himself upward with the other.

Casey had a bit of a lead on him, but it wasn't enough. Bran was closing quickly.

Tess shouted, "Hurry, Casey!"

Casey glanced back over his shoulder, watching for only a second before he resumed his climb.

"It doesn't matter if he makes it," Charisse said. "You have no prayer."

"Maybe I do," Tess said, and she twisted her weight suddenly, slipping out of Charisse's grasp and quickly slamming her shoulder into Charisse's chest.

The blow knocked her off the hood before she could regain her balance, and she crashed to the ground with a thud.

Tess heard her screech with anger, and when she looked over the edge of the vehicle, she saw Charisse sitting in a sloshing mass of mud.

"I don't believe this!" Charisse screeched.

Instead of staying focused on Tess, the other girls rushed to the side of the car and knelt by Charisse, trying to help her up.

"No!" she screamed. "Tess might—"

But Tess was already moving. She scrambled off the hood of the car in the other direction, unfurling her scarf as she moved. Dropping to the ground, she felt her feet sinking as well, but she sloshed toward the back of the car.

There, she twisted off the gas cap and began to stuff the scarf down into the narrow opening. She wasn't finished when she felt the hands closing around her. The girls were swarming over her, grabbing at her arms and her hair.

"Get her down and hold her," Charisse commanded, walking around the front of the car. With mud smeared on her dress and across her face she looked like some wild woman out of a storybook.

Before they could pin her arms, Tess pulled the lighter from her pocket.

"Get back," she warned, trying to shrug off the others.

They wouldn't release her, but she managed to spin the wheel on the lighter anyway. She prayed it wouldn't be temperamental. It had to work.

Casey could see the top of the tower. A narrow catwalk stretched around the tank, and a thin guardrail circled the metal walk.

He had only a few more rungs to go. Chill winds were swirling, biting at his face, but he tried to defy thoughts of quitting. Without looking down, he continued to pull himself upward, yanking his feet up each rung as he did. Somewhere behind him, he could hear the steady movement of Bran's feet as well.

The task was impossible, but he had to try.

He lifted his hands upward and realized he was grasping at the top rung. Drawing a quick breath, he hoisted himself on the catwalk and began to move around the tower, searching for some kind of wheel that would open the tank's contents. There had to be some kind of pressure valve or some other mechanism to evacuate the tank. Didn't there? What if the water became contaminated.

He inched along and almost slipped on the icy covering of the catwalk. After a second he managed to regain balance and keep moving.

The Christmas lights covered the top of the tank, and if there were valves he couldn't find any. He had to inch along even further to continue his search.

The catwalk vibrated slightly as Bran stepped onto it. Casey turned cautiously, gripping the guardrail as he looked back at his adversary. He'd hoped to be finished with the water business before he had to deal with an attacker, but now that wasn't possible.

He checked his watch.

Four minutes to midnight.

Bran started forward, ax over his head.

"Four minutes to midnight," Charisse taunted, and S.W. clutched at Tess's wrist, trying to claw the lighter out of her grasp.

The flame had gone out because Tess had not been able to keep her thumb on the lever which released the fuel, but she was trying to spin the wheel again.

Nancy and Serena were tugging at her legs, trying to drag her back from the car. Tess began to kick at them, but she had no way of anchoring herself to prevent their efforts. She felt her body beginning to move along the ground, the cold mud waking through her sweater and jeans.

The ax came for Casey in a wide arc, the blade gleaming like a prism in the Christmas lights. Bran's face was twisted with the determination of his effort.

Casey stood frozen, watching the movement as if it were a film spool unfurling one frame at a time. If the blow connected it would sink the blade deep into his flesh, but he couldn't move too soon. That would only give Bran a chance to react and adjust his trajectory.

The perfect moment had to be selected. Bran had to think he had an easy target.

The blade whished in the cold night air, moving closer and closer.

Casey ducked a second before it would have touched his neck, and the ax moved over his head. Bran grunted in anger when he realized he'd missed, but the force he'd put behind his swing carried the blade onward.

The hard steel crashed into the side of the water tank, the impact producing a loud clang which was picked up by the wind and swirled into the darkness.

At the same instant the blade bit through several strands of lights, severing the electrical connections and sending sparks spewing out from the tank.

Casey had hoped the swing would also penetrate the tank and let the water flow, but the structure had been built to hold the heavy weight of the water it contained. It wasn't made to cave in easily.

As Bran started to recover, Casey braced his hands against the guard rail and swung his foot out in a side kick. He aimed all his strength at Bran's midsection, and when the kick connected, Bran doubled over.

162

As a grumble of pain came up through his throat, Casey grabbed for the ax handle, but Bran didn't let it go.

Tess felt her fingers weakening. In a moment, S.W. would be able to take the lighter away. That would remove her last hope. Even if Casey succeeded somehow against Bran, there would be no way to set the blaze.

She had to do something, something fast.

She tried to come up with an idea, but then her fingers failed her, and the lighter slid from her grasp into S.W.'s

"Stop!" she screamed at S.W, even as the other girls continued to tug at her.

The scream and its intensity made S.W. pause and look into her eyes, and for a second Tess saw a glimmer of remorse. S.W. had been her friend a long time. They'd been through a great deal together; there had to be something that remained between them.

"What do you want?"

"I can't die without my new hat can I?" she asked.

The look on S.W.'s face seemed to indicate that the query had had an impact. She was thinking. Thinking about their friendship, Tess hoped.

Casey's hat had fallen only a few inches away.

"Help me!" she demanded.

S.W. hesitated, and that was all Tess needed. She pulled away from the others and grabbed for the hat. The matches were in the band where Casey had left them.

The girls had managed to tug her several inches away from the end of the scarf, but she rolled toward it, pulling out the matchbook, ripping a match free and striking it as she moved. It blazed, and she touched that match to the others in the pack, setting them all on fire.

The flame quickly shot upward, and she angled it toward the scarf. For a second she thought it would touch off the fabric, but a whip of wind pushed the flame back.

"Nooo!" Tess shouted in frustration, and with a quick lurch, threw herself forward, kicking in the same instant and managing to cover a couple of inches.

The wind swirled again, and her fingers managed to find the end of the scarf. Without hesitating, she touched the flame of the material, and it blazed.

"It's going to explode!" S.W. warned. "Get back."

"It won't be enough," Charisse said, even as the other girls curried away.

She stood near the front of the car, and as the flame crawled down the scarf toward the gas tank, she held up her hands. "You won't win."

Tess didn't listen. She turned and ran, putting as much distance between herself and the car as she could manage.

When she heard the first rumble of the explosion, she clawed forward and hit the ground, placing her hands over her head.

Beneath her, she could feel tremors, and the night was suddenly no longer dark. A moment of daylight flared, and then ear-splitting thunder.

With an arm up to shield her eyes, she rolled over and looked back toward Charisse. The flame was billowing from the car but the sorceress wasn't moving, and she seemed unaffected even though the heat from the blast should have been searing her eyelashes.

Tess felt her heart sink, and a second later she felt her hopes collapse as she saw a figure hurling off the water tower toward the ground.

Charisse seemed pleased, thrilled. She raised her arms and was about to dance about, but then the water began to pour in a steady stream.

The gushing force increased in the next second, and before Charisse could move, she was being showered with the icy spray.

Even over the roar of the blaze, Tess could hear the cries of frustration.

Charisse screamed as the water washed over her, and then she seemed to begin to melt.

Tess realized after wiping her eyes that it was not that she was shrinking. The water seemed to have softened the ground, and she was sinking into it.

"Noooooooooooot meeeeeeeee!" Charisse screamed, but the protest did little to halt what was happening.

Flames from the vehicle seemed to leap onto the ground and rush toward the witch's twisting form.

Tess realized it wasn't natural. Something odd had taken over, something beyond understanding. The flames began to circle around Charisse, and the water did not affect them. They blazed brighter than orange, becoming a hot, white light, like shimmers of lightning.

Then the earth began to rumble. She felt even stronger vibrations than before, and the ground began to split around Charisse's feet.

Her scream became a scream of terror, and Tess almost wanted to run to her, to help her as the earth swallowed her up.

Epilogue

Candles

Tess parked the Buick outside the candle store and climbed out, adjusting her jacket against the January wind. The day was sunny but the temperature was still hovering around the freezing mark.

Pushing open the door, she moved inside quickly to get out of the chill and pushed the door closed behind her.

"What a winter," Mrs. Tannenberry said from her place behind the counter. She was about to say something more when she recognized Tess.

"My goodness sweetheart, are you out and about?"

"Yes, ma'am. I couldn't stay in forever. It's been almost a month."

"I've been telling everybody it's a miracle. That you weren't killed, I mean. That old car was a death trap, shouldn't have been on the road."

"It was a good car," Tess said. "The road was just slick." Mrs. Tannenberry shook her head. "Still it was just awful what happened."

Tess selected candles from the shelf and placed them on the counter, fishing in her pocket for some cash.

Mrs. Tannenberry kept talking as she rang up the purchase.

"The car spinning out of control and slamming into the water tower. My goodness. I'd have thought it was liquor if it had been anyone else, but you I know. Some kids are so terrible. It is awful about Bran Hatten, although if he hadn't been up there vandalizing after everything else he did, he never would have gotten killed. That boy has always been trouble. Just went crazy didn't he? Too much meanness in him. His family's fault."

Tess only nodded and counted out her money when Mrs. Tannenberry extended her palm.

"Well, you be good," she said.

"I will," Tess said.

"Glad you're doing well."

"Thank you."

She pushed open the door and stepped onto the street. She was about to walk toward the car when a voice stopped her. "What have you got in the bag?"

It was Casey. He loitered near the edge of the building with his hands in his pockets. The bruises he'd received through all of the events on New Year's Eve had begun to fade.

"Just some candles," she said.

"How are you doing?"

"Okay. My nerves are settling down. My folks are letting me out of their sight."

"Think they'll let me see you again soon?"

"Soon. Once they're convinced you aren't dangerous. They're not really sure what happened. Especially since the cops are still looking for Charisse."

"They've interviewed everybody at the party, but they haven't found many answers."

"Not many, and our friends are not talking much."

"Serena, S.W., and Nancy? No, they're not. They're probably not going to prosecute them. They didn't really do anything. Bran is the one who actually killed people. Case closed."

"Have you talked to S.W.?"

"No. I don't think she can face me. I know it was Charisse's fault, but it still hurts to think about what happened. S.W. turned on me just because she thought she could be a little prettier. I may try to talk to her soon. I've learned to deal with confrontations these days."

"So where are you going with the candles?"

She bowed her head for a moment, then looked up at him, a bit embarrassed.

"I read some more. About magic and everything. Charisse said something about me having great energy. I thought I'd better explore that a little more."

"Oh?"

"Don't get any wild ideas. Just to understand. And I'm keeping in mind that Charisse had grown stronger over the years. If she somehow managed to escape again, well, it took a combo of all of the elements this time. Next time, she might be unstoppable."

"So the candles?"

"If they're burned at the site where she was consumed by the earth, they could help make sure she doesn't escape."

Casey put an arm around her shoulders. "I'll go with you then. You could probably use a hand."

"Yeah, and a lighter."

About the Author

Sidney Williams is the author of numerous novels including the Si Reardon thrillers, *Fool's Run* and *Long Waltz*. His books from Crossroad Press include the slasher thriller *Dark Hours* and the Lovecraftian action-adventure novel *Disciples of the Serpent*. Sidney's short stories have appeared in numerous publications including *Cat Ladies of the Apocalypse, Love Among the Thorns, Deranged* and the upcoming *Unknown Heroes vs. the Forces of Darkness*. Sidney's first novels were released by Pinnacle Books. Those include *Blood Hunter, When Darkness Falls* and the possession thriller *Azarius*. He wrote several YA books under the name Michael August.

A former newspaper reporter, Sidney is now an adjunct professor of creative writing. He is originally from Louisiana and spent several years in Orlando. He now resides in Virginia with his wife and their cat Zoë Moonshadow.

Visit him at SidIsAlive.com, Facebook.com/SidneyWilliamsBooks for occasional flash fiction or seek him out as Willysid on TikTok for microfiction.

Sign up for his newsletter at sidneyw.substack.com.

Curious about other Crossroad Press books? Stop by our website:
http://crossroadpress.com
We offer quality writing
in digital, audio, and print formats.

Subscribe to our newsletter on the website homepage and receive a free
eBook.

www.ingramcontent.com/pod-product-compliance
Lightning Source LLC
Chambersburg PA
CBHW022122170626
46808CB00002B/815